To Ginny

Thank you for your suppo[rt]

May you enjoy reading BRACIE as much as I enjoyed being used by God to write it

Be Blessed
and
Enjoy

Beulah Nevein

Bracie

Beulah Neveu

Abounding Favor Publishing Company
Houston, Texas

Abounding Favor Publishing Company
P.O. Box 450515
Houston, Texas 77245
713-729-7168

Copyright 2011, Beulah Neveu

All rights reserved. No part of this book may be reproduced, stored in a retrieval system, or transmitted by any means, electronic, mechanical, photocopying, recording, or otherwise, without written permission from the author.

Manufactured in the United States of America

ISBN: 978-0-9820004-2-7

Bracie

Acknowledgements

First, I would like to give all praise and honor to God for blessing me with the gift of writing. I thank the Father for blessing me with the opportunity to write my first novel.

I would like to thank my husband, Thomas, for being my inspiration and strength. I thank him for his prayers and support in my every endeavor.

I would like to thank my mother, Verna LaCour, for being my greatest example of living a life surrendered to God. I would like to thank my children Verna2, DeAnthany, DeJuan, and DeRaymond for always believing in me and loving me. I would like to thank their spouses for the love they have given my children and grandchildren. Thanks to Delores Curlin for being my example of a godly wife. I would like to thank my pastors, Dr. Gusta Booker, Jr. and Pastor Ronnie Booker, Sr. for their wonderful spiritual guidance, prayers, and for preaching the uncompromising Word of God.

I would like to acknowledge my brothers, Donald Hall and Kenneth Bilton, for encouraging me to pick up my pen and start writing. I would also like to acknowledge the ladies of Woman2Woman for teaching me the importance of having good character and the courage to stand up for what I believe. I would also like to acknowledge Pastor San Lee, Cathy Ozan, Cheryl Brown, John Wright, Jarrett McDonald, Lillian Harris, Gary and Rosalind Hicks, Romesha Hall, Casey Vinson, and Kristin Leonard for their continual encouragement and support.

Last, but certainly not least, I would like to acknowledge my grandson DeAntuan, who I believe will one day say grandma, and Annetra Piper whose smile, patience, and wisdom helped me get through the editing process.

Chapter One

Bracie sat in front of the television, not really watching it.

"There is your man, and this time he is with a woman."

She had heard the jokes many times over the years. Everyone who knew her, knew about her not so secret crush on the very rich and very handsome, Tyler Shaw.

She had admired him from afar since high school. She never said anything back then, because he was four grades behind her. Bracie, for the most part, was quiet and laid back. She wasn't in any school functions, because she had a young daughter and son to take care of. Most of her classmates were into cheerleading, being a part of the band, or in some other school function. With two children, all she could do was watch Tyler in the hallways of Madison High School. He seemed quiet and withdrawn. He was tall and handsome. He stood out because of his height and looks, but mostly, because he stayed to himself. Every girl at Madison had mentioned him at some point and time in their conversation.

Bracie graduated, and all thoughts of Tyler Shaw were left there at school.

Years later, the boy she had a crush on had become even more handsome. His 6' 4" frame looked like God chiseled it from a mold called Perfect. He had become a famous movie producer and director. He stayed secluded from the public, but Tyler Shaw's name was known by most of the women in America. One day while watching one of his movies with her family, Bracie made the mistake of saying that she once had a crush on him and would like to meet him. The jokes started that day and never stopped. That was 15 years ago.

The laughter brought her back to the family gathering.

Her son Joe'Al told her, "Ah, Mom, don't pay attention to them; they should let that go."

She smirked and said, "Yeah, they should, huh?"

Her youngest son Raymond came into the room in the middle of the joke, and when he realized it was about Bracie, he simply said "Tyler Shaw again?" This time everyone in the room laughed, including Bracie.

Everyone was gone and Bracie was left alone in her apartment to reflect back over the day. She loved her family. One daughter and three sons had given her eleven grandchildren. She loved spending time with them, but she also knew she was able to send them home. Her children had become very protective of her since Matthew passed. They were like a mother hen over her chicks. Bracie laughed at how the roles had changed. They each wanted her to come to live with them. She chose to stay on her own. She wanted to be alone, and she wanted to heal.

Bracie had loved Matthew with a passion that was hard to explain, even to herself. She thought about the first time they made love. They dated three years before they got married, but she had stood by her Christian belief that sex before marriage was not an option anymore. She had had her four children as an unwed mother. Matthew respected her for that and joined the church where she was a member. After awhile everyone at church knew they were meant to be.

She smiled at how nervous she had been on their wedding night, for she had been celibate for eight years. She thought about the gentle way Matthew had caressed her face and how softly he had kissed her lips. She kissed him back and her love for him began to wash her nervousness away. Bracie closed her eyes as she remembered his lips on her neck and the heat that raced through her body when he held her. She remembered whispering his name. The covers on the bed were already pulled back. He pulled her gown over her head. Even now, she still could not remember him getting out of his pajama pants.

Beulah Neveu

He laid her back on the bed. He began by kissing her at the top of her head. The pleasure she was feeling was incredible. She wanted to close her eyes, but was afraid she might miss something. She closed her eyes to concentrate on the ecstasy she had waited so long to feel. Bracie remembered saying "Not Yet." Matthew knew exactly what she meant and what she wanted. They stared into each other's eyes as they made love for the first time. She took her bottom lip into her mouth and bit down on it. Bracie remembered caressing his back, holding him, and touching him. He was kissing the base of her neck, when she noticed he touched a very sensitive spot.

"Oh Matthew," she had cried out. Bracie grabbed onto the sheets as her body gave way to her first real sensation as a married woman. At the age of 43, Bracie made love for the first time. Even now she cherished the memory of that night. That was the first of many more nights and days of ecstasy and passion in their marriage. All she had now were memories, and she tried not to think about them too often.

Chapter Two

"Hello," Bracie said into the phone. "Don't forget, we're going out Friday for our regular at Monterey's," Sheila said on the other end.

"I won't, actually I'm looking forward to it," Bracie said. She and Sheila were both widows. Sheila's husband Daniel passed away a year after Matthew. Bracie, Sheila, and Daniel had been friends for over 17 years. They were godparents to Bracie's children. When she introduced them to Matthew, they welcomed him with open arms. They could plainly see that he made Bracie very happy. They began bowling and going to Monterey's every Friday. After the men passed, Bracie and Sheila didn't bowl much, but they kept the Monterey tradition. This was when they caught up on things and made plans for the future.

"I'll pick you up at 7:30," said Sheila.

"See you then," Bracie said and hung up the phone. Bracie still couldn't drink; one margarita had her feeling good, so usually that's all she had.

Bracie sat down in her white high back chair. She curled her feet under, so she could think. I'll be 52 this year; what am I going to do with my life? She thought. With the money from the insurance policy, she paid her rent for a year and put the rest up. The money she made from working at a daycare, she had saved it all. She was very careful with her money, so she had a nice nest egg in the bank. Bracie looked at the clock and picked up her coffee. She had an hour before work. She liked her job, but already knew she would retire at the age of 55.

"Then what?" She said out loud. She finished her coffee and put the cup in the sink. Bracie went to get dressed. She stood in front of the floor length mirror looking at her size 14 shape. She loved it! After being a size 18-20 for over 20 years, this was a welcomed sight. Bracie turned and straightened her jacket and smiled again. "Well kids, here I come." And off she went to work.

"I'll have my regular," Bracie told the waitress.

The waitress repeated the order to be sure it was right. "Frozen margarita, nachos with chicken, and no jalapeños."

Bracie nodded. She had the same order for over five years, and they always repeated it to her. Everyone at the restaurant knew them and expected to see them on Fridays.

Bracie

"How are you?" Sheila asked.

"Fine, I can't complain. Besides, who would want to hear it?" Bracie tried to reassure her.

Sheila just looked and smiled.

"Ok, I didn't go out with Nolan. He wasn't my type," Bracie said.

Sheila shook her head. "You never gave him a chance. Bracie you will be 52 this year, and you still won't go out with anyone but John. You stay stuck in that apartment all the time."

Bracie knew she was right. All she did now was go to church, write poetry, and spend time with her family. She seemed to have no real life of her own. The waitress broke into her thoughts when she put the drinks on the table.

"Well, how is it going with you and Charles?" Bracie asked.

This made Sheila smile. "We are doing great," she said while sliding her left hand across the table. On it was a beautiful engagement ring.

"Now that's what I'm talking about," Bracie said, truly happy for her BFF. "I hope you don't wait too long, you know you are getting old."

They both laughed because Bracie was four years older than Sheila. The food came and they ate and talked about wedding plans. Bracie agreed to stand with Sheila on her wedding day. They both knew it couldn't be any other way.

Bracie was quiet on the way home.

"What's on your mind?" Sheila asked.

Bracie, knowing she could talk to her said, "I get so lonely for a companion sometimes."

They both were quiet for a moment, when Sheila said,

"I understand. I was there too, but you have to get off of that computer and get out sometimes."

Bracie laughed, for she knew that besides Sheila and John, her computer was her closest friend. They were quiet again, when Sheila asked,

"Are you still leaving messages on Tyler Shaw's fan site?" Bracie knew where this was leading, but she still told the truth.

"Yes, but this will be my last year. I promise."

"Ok, we will see," Sheila said as they drove up to Bracie's apartment. Sheila watched her go in before she drove off.

Bracie showered and lay across the bed. She couldn't sleep, so she got up and went to the computer. She checked her messages; nothing exciting was on it, yet she stayed on for about an hour. The phone rang, and she turned to look at the clock. Who is calling me at midnight, she thought.

"Hello." Bracie answered the phone slowly.

"What's up, girl?" John said.

"You scared me, but nothing's up. I just got in from Monterey's with Sheila."

John laughed and said, "You still staying stuck in that apartment? I'll be home next week and we'll go to lunch."

Bracie

Bracie agreed. "Let me know when you get in, and John…, don't try to set me up with anyone." They both laughed because she knew he would never do that.

Bracie said seriously "Be careful out there, and I'll see you soon."

John said, "Ok," and hung up. Bracie shut down the computer and sat on the side of the bed.

Bracie talked to God out loud. *"Father, thank you for John. He has been my true friend and support for so many years. Thank you for giving him shoulders strong enough for me to lean on and for letting him be wise and compassionate enough to say no and still hold on to me. Amen."* She lay down and thought about him. They had been friends for a very long time. John had been her encourager and strength for over 25 years. It took him a few years in the beginning to realize she cared for him. One night over dinner, he simply told her how much he valued their friendship, and he wanted to protect that at all costs. And he had! She knew he was letting her know he cared about her too much to sleep with her and risk ruining their friendship. They had been friends long enough for him to know and understand when she loved, she loved deeply, and she loved hard. He promised himself he would never bring her pain or heartache. Bracie thought about all the times she had cried on his shoulder. Before Matthew, it was John who held her when times were rough. He held her when that person who she thought was so special, walked out on her. It was John who held her and rocked her when Matthew passed. He loved her enough to tell her the truth at all times, even when it hurt or made her angry. He never told her "I told you so" when she didn't take his advice, which didn't happen too often. She smiled and thought, John is the kind of male friend that every female needs.

Bracie got up early so she could pray before she prepared her morning coffee. She thought about asking God for a man in her life, but decided against it. Bracie opened her Bible and all other thoughts left her mind. She wanted and needed this time with her Father for she felt so alone. When she finished praying, she went into the kitchen. It felt empty and void of life. She made her coffee and sat down at the table. Tears began to roll down her face. "What's wrong now?" she said to herself, as she picked up her coffee, and went to sit in her favorite white chair. *"Lord, I know you are with me, so why do I feel so alone?"* she asked and waited, hoping to hear an answer.

She finished and hurriedly got ready for church. She stood in front of the mirror and practiced her church smile. She didn't want anyone to know how lonely she had become. To everyone, she seemed to be a pillar of strength, but that was far from the truth.

Two weeks earlier she had run across a list she made with Matthew, and it tore at her heart. She called John. When he answered the phone, she was crying uncontrollably. He got to her as soon as he could. When she opened the door for him, she

Bracie

fell into his arms. They stepped inside, and he held her and let her cry. He never said a word; he just let her cry.

She looked into the mirror and said "He is too honorable." That was one time she wanted him to lay everything aside and make love to her. She wanted to be touched and to be held. He had never crossed that line and she knew he never would, especially when she was hurting for the man she truly loved. Bracie practiced her smile again, wiped away the tear that welled up in her eye, and freshened her makeup.

"Perfect," she said, and headed out the door.

Everyone at church knew her, so she was greeted with lots of love and smiles. She smiled back and gave out plenty of hugs, especially to the children. She went to the podium for praise and worship. She had been singing on the praise team for many years. She loved singing and took that responsibility very seriously. Oliver asked if everyone remembered "You Are Great." He had several requests for the song. It had been years since they sang it, but it was one they would never forget. Just thinking about the words to the song made her teary eyed.

"Lord please let me make it through this song," she prayed.

Church service was awesome. Rev. Roland preached from Matthew 14:22-33, and his topic was, "When Life Is Tough, Jesus Is There." She was encouraged, for life was not only tough; it had gotten so lonely. She made it through the song, but not like she wanted to. She came out alive, but her tears had washed all of her makeup away.

Aside from feeling lonely at times, life for Bracie was simple. She liked it that way or at least she said she did. Bracie loved writing poetry and won several awards for two of her poems, *True Friendship* and *I Am A Woman*. She had written *True Friendship* for John. Because most people thought they had been and were lovers again, the concept of him being a true friend to her went right over their heads. She wrote *I Am A Woman* for herself. It was the one thing she always celebrated in life; that God made her a woman. Even with the flaws and the many hats women have to wear, especially Christian women, she was ecstatic that God made her a woman.

The horn blowing brought Bracie out of her thoughts. She was going with Sheila to help finalize her wedding plans. They had a hectic, but fun afternoon. Bracie asked Sheila if she had picked out the lingerie for her wedding night. Sheila knew what that question meant; Bracie had done it for her.

"Show it to me when we get to the house," she said. They both laughed.

Bracie said, "I figured I would help by taking one thing off of your to do list."

Sheila was excited, but nervous as Bracie walked into her bedroom. She knew her friend's love of lingerie ranged from soft and sweet to wild and way out. Bracie came out of the room carrying a flowing, off white, sheer robe that covered a long satin spaghetti strap gown.

Sheila smiled. "It's beautiful."

Bracie laughed "You thought I had something wild or crazy, huh?"

They both laughed now. Sheila looked at her friend. She knew Bracie wanted someone in her life, but she also knew Bracie was afraid. She had shut her feelings down after Matthew had passed and would not let another man get near her. Sheila knew Bracie was strong and would get passed this. She had everything else. Bracie brought Sheila out of her thoughts when she handed her the gift.

"Thanks girl. Charles will appreciate it." They smiled and Bracie walked her to the door.

Bracie lay in bed that night happy for Sheila that her loneliness had come to an end.

Sheila's wedding was beautiful. Bracie stood there wondering if God would ever send her someone. She made a toast to her friend at the reception, and now Sheila was gone on her honeymoon.

Bracie sat in her favorite chair. She was alone again, for she knew her carefree days with Sheila would be limited. There was a knock on the door.

"I wonder who this could be?" she thought as she walked to the door.

Beulah Neveu

"Who is it?" she called out.

"It's me," she opened the door and let John in.

"What are you doing here this time of night?" she asked.

He gave her a hug and said, "I came to check on you."

They sat down and talked for awhile, mostly about nothing. He reached across the table and touched her face; she let him. She looked at him and tears rolled down her cheek. He came around the table and lifted her into his arms. He looked down at her and kissed her forehead.

"It's going to be alright," he finally said.

"I know," she answered back.

Bracie laid her head on his chest and held him tight. She felt safe in his arms, and he knew it. John lifted her face towards him and kissed her forehead again.

"You okay now?" he asked.

Bracie gave a slight smile and said, "Yes; how did you know I would need you?"

He smiled at her and said, "Because I'm John."

They both laughed as she walked him to the door.

"Call me if you need me, I'll be home until Wednesday."

She said, "Okay," and closed the door.

Chapter Three

Bracie sat at her computer and logged in. She saw there was a message and clicked the red tab. Did she see right? Was that Dwayne Brolin's name? She had not seen that name in over thirty-five years. They had grown up across the street from each other as kids. She had played at his house with him and his sister every day that she could remember. She'd looked forward to walking across the street each day so she could get away from the hell and unhappiness in her own home. Dwayne's front porch was where she could laugh, play, and be a kid. She and her brother played there more than they did at home. She laughed as she thought about the times they played the childhood game of mama and daddy. She had her doll, and her and Dwayne's house was on one side of the porch while her brother and his sister's home was on the other side. Bracie believed in her child's heart, that one day she and Dwayne would get married and live in a house like his mom and dad. When

Bracie's mom moved them from Third Ward, she moved Bracie's dream, too. Bracie believed after awhile that Dwayne forgot about her.

She clicked on the message, read it and laughed. It was him! She hit the reply button to write back. It had been so long, and he had not forgotten her. After she finished her reply, she hit send and smiled. She sat there for a moment to think back and decided tonight would be a short computer night. She shut the computer down and got into bed. He had not forgotten her, she kept saying to herself. That night she slept soundly.

Bracie got up early to check her messages. Dwayne had replied. She left her phone number and hoped he would call. She was at work when her wait came to an end. Her phone rang, and she knew it was him. She stepped out to take the call. "Wow, it's really him," she thought as they talked. They made a dinner date to catch up, and she could hardly wait to see him again. When she got home, she went straight to the computer. She went to Dwayne's internet social network site to take a look at his pictures. "He has a beautiful wife and daughter," she thought. She found a single picture of him to enlarge so she could see him up close. He was as handsome as she thought he would be.

By the time Thursday came, she was a nervous wreck. Besides John, this would be her first date with a man since Matthew had been gone. They agreed to meet at her brother's restaurant, Al's Spice One. She got there first and waited for him in the seating area by the door. He walked in a few minutes later. She stepped into his arms. They shared a big hug, and the waitress showed them to their table. They talked, laughed, and played catch up for over two hours. She knew it had to end, but it seemed too soon. They promised to stay in touch as they walked outside. Dwayne showed her his motorcycle. It was a beauty. He walked Bracie over to her car, where he hugged her again before she got in.

"We'll talk again soon, biker boy," she said. He agreed.

"I have to go and call my mother to tell her I saw you," he told her. They laughed and said their goodnights. She drove away happy for the first time in a long time. Bracie's cell phone went off at work the next day. She was about to go on break, so she waited a few minutes before she would check it. The message was from Dwayne saying how much he enjoyed last night. She smiled and replied that she had enjoyed last night, also. They texted each other about 20 minutes, then they had to get back to work.

Bracie invited Dwayne to dinner a few times, so he could get reacquainted with the family and meet some of the new ones. Anthany kept watch over Bracie like a CIA agent. He wanted to know why Dwayne was really coming around. He noticed that every time Dwayne's name was mentioned, his mom had a little smile on her face.

"D'john, talk to your brothers, especially that oldest one," Bracie was telling her daughter over the phone, when her sons walked up behind her.

"Talk to us about what?" All three of them said at once.

"I'll do it, they are here," Bracie said and hung up the phone. She looked at her sons and laughed. "The Three Musketeers," she thought.

"Look sons, Dwayne is a childhood friend. We haven't seen each other in years, and we are just trying to catch up on each other's lives."

"Yeah right, I remember you saying he was your first love," Anthany said to her.

Bracie smiled "I did say that, but I was referring to when we were children."

They looked at her and replied at the same time, "Whatever you say."

She was glad they had not seen the hug Dwayne had given her Sunday when she was saying goodbye. He had kissed her cheek, well, it was closer to the side of her mouth than on her cheek. She looked at him, but didn't say anything. When he drove off she touched the place where he had kissed her. She walked over to join D'john and the other ladies who were outside talking. D'john smiled at her mother as if she saw what happened. Bracie tried to convince herself that she had no emotional feelings for Dwayne. He's married, she kept telling herself.

Bracie

"Mama!" Raymond called to her. She looked at her son.

"Nothing now," Raymond said as he walked out of the door. Joe'Al stood by Bracie while Anthany watched.

"Ma, we don't want you to get hurt, that's all."

She gave a small smile and said, "I know son. Dwayne and I really are just friends. You know I can't and won't be anybody's lover. You know your mama better than that."

Anthany stepped in and said, "Mamas get lonely, too."

Bracie looked at her oldest son, but did not reply to his statement.

Lying in bed that night, Bracie kept thinking about Anthany's statement. She knew he could tell her feelings were going beyond friendship, and he wanted to protect her. Bracie lay there wondering what it would be like to kiss Dwayne. She wanted to kiss him. Would she enjoy it, would it turn her on, or would it just mess things up? Bracie knew by the age of 19 she really liked to kiss. The more she perfected the art of kissing, the harder it became to please her. She went to sleep with Dwayne on her mind. I guess mamas do get lonely, she thought.

Bracie stood in front of the mirror this Sunday with a real smile on her face. Lord help me, she thought to herself. I am so confused. I know Dwayne is married, but I can't get him out of my mind. He didn't forget me all those years.

She didn't know why that mattered so much, but it did. She was greeted at church with love as usual. Pastor Roland preached from Matthew 6:26 about not worrying and said, "God is Our Source. God is our continual and unlimited source. If he keeps the sun and moon in place, then why are we falling apart?" She heard him say more, but wasn't quite sure what. Her mind kept drifting in and out.

"How was the honeymoon?" Bracie was grilling Sheila about all the details of her honeymoon over their usual Friday night margaritas. Sheila was talking when she noticed how Bracie's face lit up when her phone messenger went off. Bracie made a reply and turned to look at Sheila's face.

"Ok, what's going on, who is he, and when did you sneak him in on me?" Sheila asked. Bracie told her about Dwayne. Sheila's smile was gone.

"Bracie, he is married and you need to be careful."

She looked at Sheila, "I know he's married, I just told you. It's not like that, besides you should know me better than that. Who I am didn't change when Dwayne came on the scene." Sheila noticed how defensive Bracie became so she let it go and changed the subject. Sheila dropped Bracie off after Bracie's second drink, which was out of character for her. Sheila said nothing, but already knew what she had to do.

Bracie sat at the computer trying to decide if she would turn it on. She got up from her desk and lay across the bed. "I just want to kiss him that's all, one simple little kiss," she said aloud. She turned over and went to sleep.

Dwayne and Bracie met at Hick's Barbeque for dinner that next Friday night. They got a table towards the back. They laughed and talked as always. Bracie told him about her poetry idea. She mentioned a poem she had written for Matthew before they were married titled 'You Touch My Soul.' She used it on the front of their wedding programs. He liked it. Dwayne touched her hand and told her to dream big and then go for it. They realized it was time to go and wondered how the time went by so fast. He got up first and pulled her chair back. Dwayne paid the tab and walked Bracie to her car. They said their usual goodbyes, but this time he didn't just hug her. Dwayne took Bracie into his arms and kissed her on the lips. She looked at him and returned the kiss. Dwayne enjoyed the taste and feel of Bracie's lips on his. He pulled her closer to deepen the kiss. When Bracie let out a soft moan, she came to herself and broke the embrace. She bit her bottom lip and looked into his eyes.

"I have to go," she said.

He touched her arm and Bracie felt like he had burned her. She touched his hand, stepped back, got in her car and drove off. Dwayne stood there; he knew he had never been kissed like that and never would again. He got on his bike and rode away.

Beulah Neveu

Bracie lay in bed; she couldn't sleep. She felt so guilty. Was it because she liked it or because she knew it was wrong? Whatever it was she still wanted to see him again.

Saturday morning a knock on the door woke Bracie up.

"Who is it!" she asked rather crossly.

"It's me," she opened the door and John walked in. He just looked at her. He wanted to feel sorry for her, but couldn't.

"What's up?" she said.

"You tell me," he replied back.

Bracie made coffee in silence.

"Breakfast?" she asked so she wouldn't have to talk.

John stood over her and lifted her chin. "Bracie you are gonna get hurt and you know it." She looked at him for a second and said, "I'm fine, I promise."

John sat in front of the coffee she had placed on the table for him.

"Bracie, you didn't tell me about him for a reason. I know you are lonely, but you have to think clearly."

She didn't say anything; she just sipped at her coffee. John looked at her wishing right now he didn't know her so well.

"You kissed him, didn't you?"

She said nothing.

"You need to stay away from him until you can handle this better."

Bracie said ok, but John already knew she would see him again. They talked for awhile and he left. Bracie was angry at

Bracie

Sheila for telling him. "I'm grown; I don't need a babysitter," she thought to herself. "I can handle my feelings for Dwayne. It was just a kiss, not the end of the world. I'll talk to Sheila later." She put the two cups in the sink, got dressed, and left.

Bracie stood in front of Dwayne. He touched her face, then her neck. She closed her eyes to the gentleness of his touch.

"Oh Bracie," Dwayne said.

They shared a long kiss. He laid her on the bed and kissed her again. She rubbed her face against his as their bodies moved together.

Bracie came out of her daydream and heard her friends talking in the background.

"Bracie, girl I know you hear me talking to you." Sheila almost screamed at her.

She bit her bottom lip and looked away, but not before John saw it.

"Sheila, Bracie and I need to talk," he said.

"I just want her to be careful!" Sheila told him.

Bracie looked at Sheila and John. "I'm 51 years old, and I know what I am doing." She tried to sound convincing.

Before Sheila could say anything else, John asked her again to leave. Sheila looked at both of them and left. They watched as she drove off.

He turned to her. "You were making love to him," he stated, not asking.

"What are you talking about; I have never slept with Dwayne."

John looked at Bracie sternly and told her, "While Sheila and I were talking you were making love to him. You moaned out loud, but you gave it away when you bit your bottom lip."

She didn't say a word.

"Bracie no matter how much you enjoy it during the act, the guilt is going to eat you up afterwards, and we both know it. It's not you Bracie, and it's not worth it."

She still didn't say anything; she sat in silence. She needed to go home and shower for she knew she had made love to Dwayne in her mind while sitting at that table.

She told John, "I'll stay away from him now; my feelings are beyond my control." He knew she meant it this time. She hugged him and left.

Bracie left a message on Dwayne's phone saying she needed space, and she would contact him soon. For the next several weeks, Bracie stayed to herself. She wouldn't take calls from Sheila or John. She wanted to be alone.

Bracie sat on the bike at the gym. She didn't know if she came more often to clear her mind or to think. She knew she couldn't continue to avoid Dwayne, they had to talk. That night, Bracie called him, and they talked briefly about the kiss they shared. They both agreed to never mention it again, but they both knew they would never forget it. For some reason it strengthened their friendship.

Bracie tried to figure out what happened. How did she let her emotions get so out of control? She had been so strong before Matthew!

Bracie sat in a hot tub of bubbles. She had candles burning and soft jazz playing on the stereo. She had run across that list again, and it made her think of Matthew. She lay her head back and thought about the weekend they house-sat for a friend. Bracie slid deeper into the water as she thought about that Sunday morning. She had gotten up looking for Matthew, when she heard him calling her from the garage. There sat the nicest Gold Wing motorcycle she had ever seen. Matthew called to her. As they stood in front of the bike, he took her head and drew her in for a long passionate kiss. She looked into his eyes and knew this would be a morning she would never forget.

Matthew had one glass of wine as always for them to share. He kissed her neck which was her weak spot. She leaned her head back and held on to his arms. She touched his chest. She smiled as he closed his eyes at her touch. Matthew reached over to a tray and picked up a large towel. He placed it across the seat of the motorcycle and sat her on it. He turned her so she could straddle the bike. He leaned her back against the passenger seat and put her hands on the bike rest at her sides and told her not to move them. They kissed as he caressed her. Bracie's body was

Beulah Neveu

on fire. She squeezed the bike rest so tight her knuckles hurt, but she didn't let go.

Bracie had to regain control of her body before she could move. Bracie got off the bike and Matthew slid in her place. Bracie kissed down his shoulder to his right arm. She loved the angel he had tattooed on his bicep. She kissed it. Matthew watched her kiss his tattoo. Now he was so glad he did not have it removed. Bracie kissed Matthew and matched him with every ounce of passion she could muster. She had never felt like this in her life.

"Oh, Matthew," she cried. He held on to her as she whispered his name. Matthew was speechless. He held on to Bracie as if for dear life. She remembered laying her head on his chest. Matthew kissed Bracie on top of her head and told her to scratch number five off the list.

Bracie sat up in the now cold water. Now she knew what happened. Matthew had taught her to love her body. He taught her passion; now her body craved it like her lungs craved air. She got out of the tub and opened her closet. Lingerie lined one side of the wall. She walked in and chose one. Passion was one of the things she had come to cherish in being a woman. Now she had to learn how to control it. That would require all of her belief and faith in God. Now she understood how powerful passion could be. She wanted it, but knew it was far from happening anytime soon. Sex before marriage still was not an option. Tonight she would learn to pray for strength.

Chapter Four

Bracie sat at her computer desk. She had not touched it in over a week and that wasn't like her. As she scrolled down the screen hitting delete, Tyler Shaw's name caught her attention.

"What? This can't be true!" she said out loud.

It was his actual email address. It had the fan mail's message attached, but it wasn't from the fan mail site. Bracie hit the reply key and wrote; *Hello Tyler, my name is Bracie Turner. I don't know how your email address got into my inbox, but I am so glad it did. I live in Houston, Texas, and I would like to meet Tyler who walked the halls of Madison High School. We attended at the same time. I know Tyler Shaw the producer has over a million people on his fan site to keep him busy, so I would like to spend time meeting the man behind it all. Please call me at 555-526-2838.*

"Please let him get this," she prayed and hit the send key. Bracie went on doing what few things made her happy. She toiled over two poems trying to decide which one she should enter into a poetry contest. The winner would go to Dallas to compete for the grand prize of $5,000, a trophy, and a trip to Chicago to read their poetry on a talk show program. "I would love that," she thought and chose to enter *Don't Judge Me* into the contest.

Sheila and Bracie didn't hang out anymore. It had been a couple of months since they had seen each other, and Sheila wondered if it was because she was married or if Bracie was still upset with her for telling John about Dwayne. Bracie was her best friend and she didn't want to see her get hurt. They talked a few times and Bracie always declined her dinner invitations. Sheila was expecting her first baby, and she didn't want Bracie to find out from someone else. She took a deep breath and knocked on Bracie's door. There was no answer. She knocked again and there was still no answer. Just when Sheila turned to walk away, Bracie opened the door. Bracie looked at Sheila and stepped aside so she could come in. Bracie sat in her white chair and curled one foot under her. Sheila sat across from her. The quietness was driving them both crazy, so Sheila spoke first,

"I'm sorry I told John about your friend; that should have stayed between us. I don't want you to be angry with me anymore."

When tears began to fill Sheila's eyes, Bracie got up and gave her friend a hug.

Bracie

"I'm not angry. I didn't know how to handle that situation, and I'm glad you intervened. I was working on feelings I hadn't dealt with in a long time." Bracie told her.

That was something she had been holding in her heart since she moved from Third Ward. Bracie pushed the thoughts aside and told Sheila she was free to still make herself at home here and if she wanted something to drink, she had to get it herself. Sheila went to the kitchen and came back with a glass of water. Bracie looked because Sheila knew where she kept soda just for her.

"Water?" Bracie asked.

"Yes, I have to drink more water for the baby." she said.

Oh, okay Bracie thought. Then she realized Sheila said baby.

They both laughed until they cried, when Bracie asked, "How did that happen?"

Sheila asked Bracie to put John on speaker phone. "Hey brother," they both said at the same time. He was glad to hear their voices together again.

"My two favorite girls, what's up?" he asked.

"You ready to be a godfather?" Bracie asked.

"Sheila! Because it better not be Bracie," he said jokingly.

They laughed and talked for awhile. John told the ladies he loved them, but he had to get back on the road.

"Be careful," they said and hung up.

Sheila stayed for a while longer. Sheila told Bracie she would be the baby's godmother as they walked to the door. They hugged and Sheila told Bracie, "Sisters for life."

"For life," Bracie agreed as she watched Sheila get into her car and back out.

It was two a.m., and Bracie could not sleep. She had already done her prayer and Bible study, so why couldn't she sleep? She was tired of tossing and turning most nights. Bracie began to think about Matthew, but got up instead. She wanted companionship with a real person, not just in her mind. She turned to the side of the bed and asked God to help her.

"I am so lonely. Father, I need you. I try to stay focused on your Word, but times like this it is so hard. Lord I desire someone of my own. Please God, there has to be something that will help me, Amen."

She lay down and curled up in her fetal position, but sleep still did not come easy.

Bracie got up early Saturday morning and went for a walk around the complex. Her phone rang and she looked to see who it was. She answered

"Hello Dwayne."

He paused then said, "I've been thinking about you. Are you ok?"

Bracie answered, "I'm doing fine."

Bracie

Hearing her voice, Dwayne wanted to pull her through the phone; he wanted to hold her and kiss her again. He got his composure back and asked if she had been going to the gym. Bracie smiled because she knew he was making small talk. Hearing his voice made her realize how lonely she was.

She needed a laugh so she said, "I'm in the gym all the time, biker boy. I have to keep this old body in shape."

They both laughed at her uncanny sense of humor and her use of the pet name she had given him.

"How is your family?" she asked.

"Everyone is fine," he replied.

They talked for a minute and Bracie said, "Well let me get off the phone. I'm walking the track, but call me again soon." They said their goodbyes and hung up.

"Father, forgive me for that small lie," she said and kept walking.

The June sun was hot as Bracie watched her grandchildren play in the pool. Anthany and Romesha invited the family over for barbeque. D'john sat next to Bracie and asked her how she was doing. Before Bracie could answer, her sons walked over to where they were sitting.

"What!" D'john said. They were up to something and both ladies knew it. Bracie's sons reached over and picked her up and threw her in the pool. Everyone laughed, especially the grandkids. Since she was already wet, Bracie swam and played water tag with her grandchildren. For awhile, she pushed her loneliness aside and enjoyed being with her family. They all got out of the pool to eat. Bracie kept a change of clothes at the home of each of her children and one set in the car. She changed clothes and sat down at the table. Romesha brought her a turkey burger, because she didn't eat beef.

"Thank you," Bracie said.

They all caught up on each other's activities since their last gathering. Bracie sat back and listened as each child took their turn talking about their children. Necia ran and got on her lap.

Anthany looked and asked, "Why are you still spoiling her cause she really is too big to be sitting on your lap."

Bracie smiled and gave her granddaughter a hug; by that time, she had a lap full of grandchildren. Everyone laughed as Romesha started taking pictures of the woman who had so many kids she didn't know what to do. That's what they called Bracie at church; she attracted children like she had a child magnet. Pastor Brooks told Bracie it was her humble spirit that attracted children, that and she had a loving spirit like her mother. Bracie smiled because she knew she had now passed that loving spirit and magnet on down to D'john.

Chapter Five

Bracie walked in from getting her mail. She was sitting it on the table when the phone rang.

"Hello," she said.

"May I speak with Bracie Turner?"

Oh, my God, it's him, she thought as she sat down.

"This is she, may I help you?" She tried to sound as calm as possible.

"I don't know yet. I'm calling about an email you sent. You did send me an email," he said.

"Yes, I did send you an email."

Before she could say anything else, he asked her what would she like to do about dinner, because he would be in Houston on the second Friday of this month. Tyler sat there with the phone, waiting to see what crazy request she would make.

Bracie, now calm, said, "I would like to cook for you. I don't want to go to a restaurant because it would be a media frenzy."

Tyler asked, "Would that bother you?"

Bracie replied "It would be difficult to get to know you with people trying to take your picture and get your autograph. If you don't mind, I would like to have dinner with just you, no cameras, no press, just Tyler." He laughed at the idea and took her information. Before they hung up, Bracie asked Tyler for a big favor and hoped he would not be offended.

"What is it?" he asked.

"Can you come in a regular car? I think a limo would draw attention."

Tyler laughed and said, "I think I can honor that request, I'll see you then."

They both hung up and wondered what they had just done.

Bracie didn't know how she made it through the week. She went through that Friday on a shaky cloud. She had to cancel Monterey's with Sheila and go to the store. Bracie set the table for two. She was pleased with her meal of baked chicken, potatoes, green beans, and cornbread. She had Kool-Aid in the refrigerator and chocolate cake on the counter. She showered and dressed in a beautiful blue sundress her mom bought for her on a trip to Mexico. Bracie brushed her hair into a single ponytail and put on some lip gloss. She went into the living

Bracie

room and sat in her favorite chair. She looked at the clock and thought, it is 6:50 p.m.; maybe he will change his mind and won't show up. A knock at 7:00 p.m. sharp broke into Bracie's thoughts. She looked through the peep hole and opened the door. She smiled and welcomed him in. Tyler looked around and smiled at how comfortable her home felt. Bracie led Tyler to the kitchen and pulled back his seat. Tyler sat down and she fixed him a hefty plate and set it in front of him. She fixed her own plate and poured them both a glass of Kool-Aid and sat down. They enjoyed most of the meal in silence. She noticed he kept looking around, but didn't say anything. Tyler emptied his plate and asked for seconds. Bracie smiled and told him the food was on the stove, and he could help himself. Tyler looked at her

"You want me to get it?" he asked.

She laughed at him and answered, "If you want to eat, then yeah."

Tyler got up, put more food on his plate, and sat back down.

After dinner the two of them sat in the living room. Bracie asked Tyler what made him call her. She was surprised by his answer.

"You wanted to meet Tyler, the man who used to go to Madison," he said.

"I graduated your freshman year," she told him.

Tyler left Houston the summer after his freshman year. He moved to New Orleans with his grandparents. Because he finished high school there, the public automatically assumed he was from New Orleans.

"I wanted to meet someone who actually knew me from here," he said.

They talked and laughed; they drank Kool-Aid, and ate cake. They were enjoying themselves when Tyler's phone buzzed. He stepped into the kitchen to take the call. He hung up and sat back down. "That was my driver; he'll be here in 10 minutes." They both lost track of time, because it was now 9:50 p.m. At 10:00 p.m., sharp his phone buzzed again.

Tyler answered and said, "I'll be down in a moment," and hung up.

Bracie thanked him for coming. He hugged Bracie and told her he had enjoyed the evening. He thanked her for the wonderful meal. Bracie walked him to the door.

"Tyler you are always welcomed to come and visit." She touched his hand lightly and told him to call her whenever he could. He agreed he would.

"Thank you again," he said as he hugged her once more and left.

Bracie closed the door behind Tyler and locked it. Her shaky cloud was now strong and stable. She had had dinner at her home with Tyler Shaw and that was news she didn't want to share with anyone just yet.

Bracie

Shanelle, Tyler's assistant, was waiting for him at the studio Monday morning. She had been his right hand for years. She was with him when he produced his first movie.

"Well, how did it go?" she asked.

Tyler smiled and told her about the evening. Shanelle laughed when he told her Bracie made him get his own second helpings.

Shanelle asked more seriously, "Did she take any pictures of you or did anyone just show up?"

Tyler looked at her and simply said, "No."

They were both pleasantly surprised.

Then she asked, "Are you going to call her again?"

Thinking he would say no, she was shocked when he said, "I'm thinking about it," and went to his office.

Shanelle stood there for a moment. She had to find out more about this woman named Bracie Turner.

Tuesday evening Bracie checked her email. She had a message from Tyler. It read, *'Hello Bracie, I would like to thank you again for a wonderful evening. I will call you soon, Tyler'*. She read it a few more times and hit delete.

"I bet you will," she said with some skepticism. She got into bed and couldn't help but go to sleep with some new dreams on her mind.

Bracie closed her eyes and said, *"Lord please let him call again,"* and went to sleep.

Bracie sat under the hairdryer at her sister's hair salon. It was Francine's line of Heavenly Hair products that gave Bracie a healthy head of hair again. After Matthew passed, Bracie's hair began to thin and fall out. Everyone knew it was from the stress of Matthew's death, yet no one could stop it from getting worse. Bracie went to her sister, and within two weeks she noticed a change for the better; she had not used anything else on her hair since. Bracie believed her hair was a part of her glory in being a woman, so she took great pride in its health and beauty. Francine noticed her sister did not have the look of sadness that had shadowed her face for over two years. Before, even when Bracie smiled she could see the sadness in her eyes. Today the sadness was gone. Francine got Bracie from under the dryer and told her to sit in the styling chair. She didn't want to pry, but she had to know what happened to her sister since her last visit.

She asked, "How have you been, and what has you glowing so?"

Bracie told Francine she met up with a friend from high school, and they had gone on a very nice date. Before she got too excited, Bracie told her they might not see each other again, but it was enough to let her know she needed to start living again. That was fine with Francine, she loved her little sister and wanted her to be happy.

Chapter Six

It had been almost a month, and Bracie had not heard any more from Tyler Shaw. She wished he had not told her he would call, for she had expected one by now. She went to Wednesday Bible Study and stayed for praise team rehearsal. They went over a few old songs and started preparing for a new song for the second Sunday in July.

It was 10:30 p.m., and Bracie did not get on the computer. As soon as she lay down and got comfortable, the phone rang. She assumed it was John and answered.

"What's up dude?"

Tyler laughed and said, "Bracie?"

"Oh I'm sorry, I thought you were someone else," she said recognizing the voice right away.

"I'm sorry it took me so long to call, but I have been running on a hectic schedule," he said apologizing to her.

Bracie told him she understood he was busy and asked, "How are you doing?"

"Fine, just tired," he said, "well Bracie I'm calling because I need some of that crafty Kool-Aid you made." They both laughed.

"Well, Tyler, you are welcome to come have crafty Kool-Aid whenever you like," Bracie said with a giggle. Tyler's reply left her speechless for a moment.

"I was hoping you would say that, is Saturday ok?"

"Ok for what?" she asked.

Tyler told Bracie he would be in Austin, Texas Saturday morning for a meeting, and he would like to have a late lunch with her.

"Hello?" he said.

"Oh, I'm sorry, I had to think for a second, but Saturday will be fine."

Tyler suggested picking something up to eat on his way over. Bracie wouldn't hear of it and said she would prepare lunch herself, and she would make sure she had his crafty Kool-Aid on hand. They laughed and talked for awhile.

Tyler soon said, "I won't keep you any longer since it's after midnight." Bracie looked at the clock and couldn't believe they had been on the phone for that long.

"Goodnight Tyler, I will see you Saturday."

"Goodnight," he replied.

"Bracie," he said her name before she hung up.

Bracie

"No lights, no cameras, no press, just us," he said.

"I promise," she said and hung up the phone. Now she couldn't sleep, this time for a very good reason.

Friday night, Sheila and Bracie sat at Monterey's. Both ladies passed on their regular margaritas. Sheila knew why she passed on her drink, but wondered why Bracie passed on hers. When she asked, Bracie only said she didn't want one tonight. Bracie noticed Sheila had a little baby bump. She put her hand on Sheila's stomach to see if the baby would move. They felt a slight kick, and they both smiled. They talked about the baby and how Charles was spoiling her. Sheila asked Bracie if she could go look at baby furniture with her tomorrow. Bracie declined, but quickly said they would do it soon.

Sheila dropped Bracie at home and watched her go in. Bracie was so glad the baby kept them focused on something besides her and her life. She walked in the kitchen and set the table. Tyler will be here tomorrow. She turned the light off and went to bed. For the first time in a long time, both ladies were happy and it showed.

Bracie slept in and got up around noon. She looked forward to her day with Tyler and to being with her family tomorrow. They would have 4th of July at Andre' and D'john's home. The meal was already planned, and Bracie had her usual assignment for family gatherings. She had to bring green beans, banana pudding, and a cake of her choice. Her cake of choice this time was pineapple, D'john's favorite. Bracie chose another dress her mom bought for her while in Mexico. It was a two-tone yellow and orange sundress. Her hair was down and pulled back on one side with a yellow and orange flower clip. She had on ivory accessories and yellow and orange sandals. She stood in front of the mirror, pleased with her appearance. A knock at the door made Bracie jump. She looked through the peephole and opened the door. Tyler stood there with a dozen of roses in his hands.

"Come in." She stepped aside so he could enter.

When she closed the door, he gave her the vase and said, "These are for you." Bracie had not expected this and the surprise showed on her face. She took a deep sniff of the dark red roses and put them on the table by her favorite chair. Tyler looked at Bracie and complimented her on her outfit and her hair.

"Hungry?" she asked him.

"Very," he said as he walked to the kitchen and sat at the table. Tyler laughed within at how at home he felt. Bracie sat a glass of Kool-Aid in front of him, and they both laughed. Today she prepared grilled turkey patties, steamed veggies, wild rice, and a salad with wheat rolls. She put the dressings on the table in front of him. He looked at her strangely when she poured Ranch and French dressing on her salad. She laughed at the look on his face and told him she didn't really care for plain dressing. They talked a little, while they ate their meal. When Tyler emptied his plate, he already knew he had to get his own second helping. He refilled his plate and sat back down while Bracie refilled their Kool-Aid. They finished the meal with a slice of apple pie her mother baked.

They went to sit in the living room. Tyler noticed Bracie went straight to the white chair. Before she sat down, she took another sniff of the roses and openly admired their beauty. Tyler sat and watched her with a smile on his face.

"I'm glad you like them," he said to get her attention.

She sat down and said, "They are my favorite, all roses are. Thank you so much." They laughed and talked, and both soon realized they each had a great sense of humor. Bracie watched him as he laughed at something she said. She never gave it a second thought that he was doing the same to her. They went back to old times at Madison. They compared teachers and subjects. Tyler told Bracie how happy he had been when he went to live with his grandparents. She saw the pride in his face when he talked about them. It was his grandmother who had taught him about salvation through Jesus Christ. Bracie noticed his glass was empty and got up to refill it.

"Thank you," he said. She just smiled and sat back down.

They were laughing once again when her phone rang.

"Hello,... I'm good,... to the mall,... no I don't want to go,... I'm working on my poems for the contest,... no son, if I win here I will need two poems for the contest in Dallas,... no, I have already won awards with those two so I want to try something new… I love you, too." Bracie finished the conversation and hung up.

"I am sorry about that. It was my son wanting me to go to the mall."

"So what's with the poetry?" he asked.

Bracie told Tyler about the contest and the prizes. "The winners from here will be chosen on September 11th, the weekend of my birthday, and then go on to compete in Dallas, Texas for the grand prize the weekend of November 12th." Tyler saw the pride in her eyes as she talked about her poetry.

"I have two on the wall," she pointed to where they hung.

Tyler asked if he could look at her work. They walked over to where the framed poetry was mounted on the wall along with the ribbons she had won. Tyler stood behind Bracie while he read the poems. "My God, he smells good," she thought. She noticed how tall he was over her and that seemed exciting to her. Tyler noticed the light flower scent Bracie was wearing. It was the same scent she left on his shirt the last time he came over. He noticed how short she was and wondered what it would be like to kiss her.

"Well?" Bracie's voice brought him back to her poetry. They sat back down and he told her his thoughts on her poems. Tyler was caught off guard by her humbleness. Wanting to take the attention off of herself, Bracie told Tyler that her oldest son writes poetry also.

"His is a bit more intense," she said.

Bracie

"Intense?" Tyler asked. She nodded her head and bucked her eyes; they both laughed as Tyler seemed to get her meaning. He watched Bracie as she reached over and took one rose out of her arrangement. She took a deep breath of the flower's fragrance. At one moment, it seemed as if she forgot Tyler was sitting there.

Both seemed startled when Tyler's phone buzzed. He answered, said a quick okay and hung up.

"My driver is downstairs," he said.

They both stood and Tyler gave her a big hug. This time the hug was tighter; it wasn't the polite little hug he had given her before. Bracie hugged him back. On the way to the door, she picked up the single rose she had taken out earlier.

"For you," she said.

He looked down into her eyes and said, "Thank you, I'll call you soon, and it won't take as long this time." As Tyler walked passed her, he stopped and asked, "So when is your birthday?"

Bracie smiled and told him September 8th. He smiled and went downstairs. His driver got out and opened Tyler's door. She was surprised when he got in the front seat. She stood on the porch and watched as they drove off.

As Bracie turned to go inside, her neighbor stepped outside and asked excitedly, "Was that Tyler Shaw at your apartment? That looks just like Tyler Shaw!"

Bracie looked at Dianne and said, "Come on now, Tyler Shaw here?"

Dianne thought about it, and they both laughed and went into their separate homes.

"Well God, I didn't lie," Bracie thought.

She walked pass the roses and smiled on her way to her bedroom. She changed clothes and noticed the scent of Tyler's cologne was in her dress. She hummed as she cleaned up and started on her cake and banana pudding for tomorrow.

"What now?" she thought aloud, but this time it was for a very different reason indeed.

Church attendance was low, but the service was very good. It seemed God's presence rested upon the church the moment the praise team started singing. Bracie cried during the entire service. She felt thankful to God that He had begun to remove the heavy load of loneliness off of her heart. She felt free, and she knew it was all by his grace and mercy. He chose Tyler as his vessel, but the touch was from God. Her pastor preached from Psalms 119:105 and Jeremiah 29:9; his topic - The Word of God. He told the congregation "God's Word brings healing in all of life's situations; no study book can take the place of God's Word, and God's Word helps us feel secure in times of darkness." Bracie listened to his sermon for she knew it was God's Word that had kept her in her dark hours. That darkness seemed to be coming to an end, and she was glad. A few of her friends noticed her smile was genuine, because they could see it in her eyes. As Bracie was getting into her car, Gloria stopped

Bracie

her. She wanted Bracie to know she was glad to see her happy again. Bracie thanked her and got in her car to leave.

Bracie stopped by to see John. She pulled into the driveway and got out. She knocked and gave his mother a hug when she answered the door. John came from the back speaking on the way to the front.

"Hey girl," he said in his loud, happy voice. They stepped outside. They hugged and talked for awhile. He looked at his sister/friend and saw the radiance glowing in her face. He didn't intrude because he knew that if she needed his advice she would ask. He also knew Dwayne was not the reason for the happiness that showed on her face. Bracie told John she had to get going because she had some of the dinner and dessert for the family in her car.

He smiled at her and asked, "Where is my dessert?"

Bracie reached into the car and pulled out a bowl of banana pudding she made just for him. She gave him a hug and got into the car.

"Happy looks good on you," he said. John reached into the car and kissed her on the forehead. He stood there and watched her drive off. He said a quiet prayer as he walked in the house.

"Lord, please protect her heart and let this be good for her."

Food and fun was always center stage at their family gatherings. Bracie saw some of her nieces and nephews that she had not seen in awhile. Her oldest grandson Trevion walked up and gave her a hug. She could not believe he was a senior in high school and LeAndre' a junior. As she thought about him, he walked up also.

"Hey grandma, what's up," LeAndre' said.

Bracie could not believe his voice had gotten so deep. "I just talked to that boy a few days ago," she thought. All three walked into the house with a dish in their hands. Bracie walked over to her mom and gave her a kiss on the cheek and a hug. They looked at all the food that was prepared for today. She, her mom, and her sisters started putting the food out on the tables when Romesha began taking pictures.

"Besides Bracie, that girl takes more pictures than anyone I know," said Randy. Bracie's middle sister, Francine, walked up and all four ladies took a picture together. They were a close-knit family and everyone knew it.

JeKeith heard his grandmother's voice and came into the kitchen. He stood in front of her and smiled. Bracie reached over and gave him a hug.

"Say grandma," she told him. She placed his fingers over her lips and said grandma again. He'd started saying words about a year ago, and Bracie knew one day he would say grandma. Every chance she got, she would practice with him. She placed his fingers over her lips again, and JeKeith gave her a smile that melted her heart each time she saw it. Bracie mingled in with all her family and they all noticed how lighthearted she was. Necia ran over and gave her grandmother a hug and kissed

Bracie

her on the head. Bracie sat next to her mom, and they watched the love and happiness that was very strong in their family.

All of the ladies were in the kitchen talking when Bracie's phone rang. She looked at the number and smiled.

"Excuse me," she said and all eyes glanced her way.

Francine and Randy looked at each other and then Romesha and D'john. They all agreed whoever this was, they were glad he made Bracie happy.

"When are we going to meet him?" They asked each other.

Ms. Deanie told them all to be patient, it will happen in due time. While the ladies talked, Bracie was being watched by her sons, especially Anthany. Bracie stepped outside as she answered the phone.

"Hi," she said. Bracie was sure her smile had gone through the phone.

Tyler told her, "Happy 4th. I forgot to tell you yesterday."

He had not told her on purpose so he could call her today.

"The same to you," she said and they talked for a while. Before they hung up, Tyler told Bracie to save his number in her phone. "Now you can call me sometimes," he told her.

Tyler hung up his phone and turned to see Shanelle standing there. She didn't want to say anything negative because she could see a glow on his face that she had not seen before.

"Tyler, be careful, get to know her better."

He knew she was concerned about him so he told her, "She's good, Shanelle. There's something about her spirit that shines through, so you know right away she is a good person with a good heart."

Shanelle was concerned because Tyler had just given Bracie his private number and didn't care to mention it to her. He put his arm around her shoulder, and they walked outside.

Chapter Seven

It took every ounce of strength Bracie had, not to call Tyler before ten days. She had to purposely keep her mind occupied with other thoughts, besides him. She attended Bible Study and was glad she did, although she had not missed in over two years. The praise team had rehearsal for Sunday, and Oliver told them they had been invited to sing two songs for a Praise and Worship Summit on July 31st. Everyone agreed they would participate. Bracie got home and showered. She already knew she would not wait another day to call Tyler. She dialed his number and his voice mail picked up; she left a message and hung up. She was a bit disappointed and couldn't sleep. She chose a book to read and got into bed. Within minutes her phone rang. She looked at the number and answered.

"Hello, Tyler."

He was as glad to hear her voice as she was to hear his.

"How are you lil' lady, and why did it take you so long to call?"

Bracie explained she knew he was busy, and she didn't know when it would be a good time to call him. Tyler told her he would accept that for now, and they both laughed. He figured tonight would be as good a time as any to ask her to spend the weekend with him. Bracie was talking when Tyler cut her off.

"Bracie, would you like to spend the weekend with me in the Bahamas, the last of this month?" Did she hear right?

"Will you repeat that, please?"

Tyler told Bracie what he had just said and added, "We will have separate rooms."

He didn't want to scare her away by giving her the wrong idea. He explained he would be there on the 19th and would finish filming on the 27th. I will need two days to tie things up until I get back to the States.

A weekend in the Bahamas with Tyler. She thought about that for a moment and said yes.

"Carl will pick you up at 2:00 p.m. on Friday the 30th, and he will have your flight arrangements."

"Who is Carl?" she asked.

Tyler laughed, "I'm sorry, Carl is my driver. Bracie, I promise you will enjoy it."

"I'm sure I will," she replied. They talked until she realized it was after 1:00 a.m. She didn't want to hang up, but knew she had to face fifteen 3-year-olds and she would need all of her

Bracie

energy for work. They said their goodbyes, and Bracie went to sleep excited.

Carl was there to pick her up at exactly 2:00. He took her suitcase and opened the back door for her. She didn't want to be chauffeured and asked if she could sit in the front. When they arrived at the airport, Carl escorted Bracie to Tyler's private plane. She stood there for a moment and looked at Carl, and then the plane.

"It's okay, Ms. Turner. Tyler will be waiting for you at the airport there."

"Thank you," she said and took a deep breath as she walked towards the plane. She stopped when a young lady stepped into the doorway and spoke to her by name and to Carl.

He smiled at her and introduced them. "Ms. Turner, this is Shanelle, Tyler's personal assistant."

Shanelle welcomed her aboard and showed her to a set of seats that looked like they belonged in someone's home.

"The plane will take off in a few minutes so make yourself comfortable," she said. Shanelle and Carl talked for a moment and he left.

Bracie sat in silence taking everything in and hoping her fear of flying wasn't showing. Shanelle sat in a seat across the aisle. The pilot came over the speaker and told them to be seated and put on their seatbelts; they were about to take off. As the plane went down the runway and took off into the sky, Bracie grabbed her seat so tight she thought her fingers would break. The plane leveled off, and the pilot said it was okay to move around. Shanelle walked over to Bracie and told her it was okay to get up. Bracie looked up at Shanelle, still somewhat terrified of being so far off the ground. Shanelle took her by the hand and told her it was alright. Bracie had to get her balance as she walked to the lovely dining area. She looked in the mini fridge and got a Sprite. Shanelle sat down and offered Bracie the seat across from her. They started talking about nothing in general until Shanelle asked Bracie about her life. Bracie didn't mind talking about her family and friends. Shanelle laughed as Bracie told her some of the crazy things her children and grandchildren had done. She told her about church and how painful it had been when she lost Matthew. Shanelle shared some of her life with Bracie also. She told Bracie she and Tyler became friends when he moved in with his grandparents. Tyler left to go to college and asked her to be his assistant when he made it into the production business. They shared a few personal stories and by the time they made it to the airport in the Bahamas, Bracie had won Shanelle's heart without even trying.

Bracie and Shanelle walked into the airport lobby looking for Tyler. He saw them as they headed his way. He gave each lady a hug and kissed Bracie on the cheek. They got their bags and got into a limo that was waiting for them. They pulled up in front of a very large and beautiful hotel. They were shown to their rooms and Bracie looked at the large room trying to take everything in. Tyler took her by the hand and led her to one of the closed doors.

"This is your room," he said as he opened the door to pure luxury. Bracie stood there for a moment to take it all in. "My room is over there and the restroom is there." He pointed to the other two doors that were closed.

Shanelle and Tyler were in the sitting area when she came out of her bedroom.

"It's late evening so how about dinner and an early night?" Tyler said. Both ladies agreed and they went to dinner in the hotel's restaurant. They enjoyed dinner and Shanelle bid them goodnight. It was just the two of them now. They talked about the flight and how they spent their fourth of July.

While Bracie and Tyler were enjoying their conversation, her children were looking for her. Sheila had gone to pick Bracie up for Monterey's and could not find her. Sheila called D'john, and she called her brothers. They all called Bracie's phone, and they all got the same results - it went straight to her voice mail.

"We can't call the police because it hasn't been 24 hours, and she is grown," said D'john. They sat there wondering, where could she be? It was not like Bracie to go anywhere without letting at least one of her children know where she was going.

Tyler asked Bracie about her children, and she nearly choked on the soda she was drinking.

"I need to call them," she said.

Tyler asked for the house phone and asked Bracie for the number. When the phone rang, he passed it to her.

D'john looked at the strange number on her phone and answered.

"Hey," Bracie said softly, because she knew her children would be frantic by now. D'john told her mom to hold on so she could put her on speaker phone. Anthany asked his mom as calmly as possible

"Where are you?"

She took a deep breath and said, "In the Bahamas."

"You are where!" they all said at the same time.

Bracie explained she was with a friend, she forgot to call on the way to the airport, and she would be home late Sunday night.

"Who is this friend that has you sneaking off without telling anyone?" Anthany asked. She could tell in his voice he was not happy about not knowing who she was with.

"I am not sneaking, son. I am the mother, remember?" Bracie's remark did not faze her son in the least.

"And how long have you been knowing this friend that we know nothing about?" he asked annoyed.

"I'll see you Sunday night when I get home," she answered him and said goodnight.

Bracie

Tyler looked at the expression on Bracie's face and asked if everything was ok. She told him about Anthany and shook her head. Tyler lifted her face so she could look at him and told her, "Your son loves you, and he only wants to protect you."

"I know," she said with a smile. They enjoyed a light dessert and went upstairs. They sat and talked in the room for a while. Tyler could see Bracie was tired; he walked her to her door and told her goodnight.

Shanelle was telling Tyler goodbye when Bracie walked out of her bedroom.

"Sorry, I didn't mean to interrupt you," she said feeling a bit jealous. This was a new emotion for her, and it felt strange. Shanelle walked over to Bracie and gave her a hug. She was on her way back to the States. She had enjoyed Bracie's company and understood why Tyler liked spending time with her. Tyler stood in the kitchenette and asked Bracie what she would like for breakfast.

"Coffee and two slices of toast," she answered.

That's all? he motioned and she nodded yes. Bracie didn't realize how nice she looked with her hair down over the soft blue robe and gown she had on. Tyler kept watching her when he thought she wasn't looking. A knock on the door meant their breakfast had arrived. They ate mostly in silence and only talked on general subjects. Bracie asked Tyler what was on the agenda and how she should dress. Comfortable was all he said and waited to see what that meant to her.

Bracie stepped out later wearing light green Capri pants, a green plaid sleeveless blouse, light green and silver accessories, and silver sandals. Her hair was pulled back into a single ponytail with a green bow. Tyler looked at her and smiled. She blushed under his observation. It has been a long time since I have seen a woman actually blush, he thought to himself.

"You ready?" he asked.

Bracie stuck her arm under his, and they headed out the door. Tyler and Bracie went on a boat ride and then ate lunch at a beachside restaurant. Bracie remembered her praise team engagement and asked Tyler for the nearest phone. He reached in his pocket and pulled out a different phone than the one he usually used.

"My business phone," he told her.

Bracie called Oliver and explained she would not be able to attend the performance tonight. She felt better when he told her to enjoy her time away because everyone else would be there. Bracie hung up and took Tyler's hand.

They walked and looked through shop windows and went into a few just to look around. It was getting late, but neither wanted to go back to the room. They took their shoes off and walked on the beach holding hands. They talked some, they laughed some, and sometimes they listened to the sound of the ocean as they enjoyed the time they were spending together.

Bracie

"It's time to go in," Tyler said. They walked back to the hotel in silence. He asked Bracie if she wanted to eat downstairs or order from room service. She chose room service, for she wanted to spend as much time as she could with him while this dream lasted. She looked at the menu and ordered a sandwich and chips. Tyler put his order in, and they went to shower and change.

When their food arrived, Bracie could smell the aroma of Tyler's food from under the door. Tyler set the table. When Bracie entered the room, he stood and pulled out her chair for her to sit down. He took a deep breath of the flower scent she had on. Bracie couldn't believe Tyler was eating so much food this late, while he couldn't believe this was all she was eating.

"Sorry I didn't bring some of that Kool-Aid you like so much."

They both laughed because they knew it was the one thing that would make the meal perfect. They cleaned the table and put everything away. Tyler told Bracie they would be leaving at noon. She said she would be dressed and ready to go. He reached over, kissed her on top of her head, and said goodnight.

Tyler and Bracie sat on the plane waiting for it to take off.

"Why did you tell your family you would be home Sunday night?" he asked Bracie.

She told him all four of her children and their spouses would be at her house to see who had taken her away without their knowledge.

He looked somewhat surprised and asked, "You haven't told them you are with me?"

Bracie laughed at the look on his face and answered "No, I have not told anyone it is you. I want to enjoy Tyler alone. Once they know, they will lose sight of the man I enjoy. I know it sounds crazy, maybe even selfish, but that's how I feel."

He took her hand and told her he understood what she was saying. She squeezed his hand as the plane took off.

Carl met them at Hobby Airport and drove them to Bracie's apartment. Tyler helped take her bags upstairs. She offered him a glass of Kool-Aid; he accepted and sat at the kitchen table. He told Bracie he would be busy reviewing the movie he just finished.

"I promise to call as soon as I can," he said. Tyler touched Bracie's hand as she reached out to open the door. He kissed the inside of her hand and sent chills from her head to her toes. She looked up, and he touched her chin and kissed her softly on the lips.

"I had a great time and we will talk soon," he said in almost a whisper.

Bracie

Bracie watched him go down the stairs and get into the car. She stepped inside and closed the door when someone knocked. She opened the door for Dianne.

"Girl, where have you been? Sheila came by Friday looking for you and I told her you left in a blue Audi with a man. I told her you had luggage so you might be gone for a few days. Where did you go?" she said everything without taking a breath.

Bracie looked at her and said with a smirk "Thank you, Dianne. It's nice to know you are watching out for me."

"Anytime," she said as she walked back to her own apartment.

How about all of the time? Bracie thought to herself and giggled.

Tyler found time to call Bracie at least three times a week. She loved hearing his voice, but could tell he was tired most of the time, so she wouldn't let him stay on the phone long. The Friday before Labor Day, Bracie's phone rang. She looked at the number and answered with a smile on her face

"Hello, Mr. T."

"You busy?" he asked.

"I'm never too busy to talk to you," she answered.

"Well, open the door." Tyler said.

Bracie ran to the door and opened it. When Tyler came in she was so glad to see him, she hugged him. He hugged her back and the scent of flowers filled his nose. *God, I love smelling her*, he thought to himself.

"Happy Birthday!" he told her while putting a small bag in her hand. Before she could open it, Tyler stepped outside the door and came in with a beautiful bouquet of yellow and white roses. Bracie put the bag down and walked toward Tyler and the roses. He put the vase on the table and watched Bracie as she seemed to sniff every single rose. Tyler got her attention and gave her the bag again. She took a box out of the bag and opened it. Bracie didn't react to the emerald and diamond necklace the way Tyler expected. She looked at it again and put the top back on it. She took Tyler's hand and put the box in it.

"Thank you Tyler, it really is beautiful, but it's not me. I don't have anywhere to wear something like that."

Tyler put the box back in the bag and asked Bracie if she was sure she did not want the necklace. She stopped admiring her roses long enough to tell Tyler to hold on to it; if ever they were to go to a ball she would wear it then.

They talked over a glass of Kool-Aid, and Tyler had to leave. He gave her a hug and a kiss and left baffled with the bag in his hand.

Shanelle walked into Tyler's kitchen and saw the box on the counter.

"What's this? Bracie didn't like the necklace? What did she want?" she asked. Shanelle looked at Tyler in disbelief when he told her Bracie's reaction to the jewelry and then to the roses.

Bracie

"It's not a joke," he said,

"You had to see her with those roses. It was good to see someone appreciate the true things in life."

"Who are you giving roses and jewelry to?" asked Greg as he walked into the kitchen. Shanelle didn't say anything. She looked at Tyler when he said, "Her name is Bracie." Greg looked at the two of them and asked how long has this been going on?

"Long enough," Tyler said and walked out of the kitchen.

He turned to Shanelle "Why wasn't I told about this Bracie woman?" He demanded of her. Shanelle answered on her way out of the kitchen "Because Tyler is a grown man and he can do what he pleases, and see your way out."

"I turn my back for a second, and he finds another tramp to try and take him for all he has," Greg said to himself and left angry at Tyler and Shanelle for keeping him in the dark.

Chapter Eight

Bracie was one of the three chosen to advance on to Dallas for a chance at the grand prize. Her family was very excited for her. They all chose to go to her apartment to celebrate. D'john and Romesha noticed the roses right away.

"Those are beautiful, who gave them to you?" they asked.

It seemed everyone stopped to hear the answer.

Bracie only said, "A friend."

Raymond, being funny, said in his whiny voice "I got these lil' ole roses here from Tyler Shaw." Everyone in the room laughed, including Bracie, but for a very different reason. Ms. Deanie knew her daughter well. She saw the glow in her eyes when they were talking about Tyler Shaw. She could see the love and warmth in Bracie's face and told her daughter, "Be careful."

Bracie looked at her mom, nodded ok, and mingled in with the rest of the family.

Bracie

Tyler asked Bracie to join him for the weekend in California. He wanted to spend time with her because he had not seen her since before her birthday. Carl picked Bracie up Friday afternoon and drove her to the airport. This time she would be flying alone, so she used this time to go down her checklist. She called Sheila first and told her not to have the baby until she got back to Houston. Bracie called her mom and D'john, and told them she would be gone for the weekend and would be home Monday afternoon.

Shanelle and Tyler met Bracie at the airport. When Bracie saw Carl, she looked startled. "Oh, he flew in the front," Shanelle laughed.

They all got in the car, and Carl drove them up to a beautiful mansion. Bracie looked at Tyler when he said, "Welcome to my home."

They were greeted by Greg inside the house. Tyler and Shanelle said "Dang!" at the same time, just not out loud. Tyler introduced them and he could tell right away, Greg had something negative to say. Bracie didn't notice the way Greg cut his eyes at her, for she had her focus on Tyler.

"Show Ms. Turner to her room, please Cora, thank you," he told the young lady standing at the bottom of the staircase.

Greg asked Tyler. "How can you invite a strange woman into your home? She will know what you have and what she can get out of you."

Tyler told him in a very stern tone, "This is my house and I invite whom I please. Now if you don't mind I have company." Tyler walked away and Greg walked out.

Shanelle knocked on Bracie's door and went in when she heard her voice.

"This room is beautiful," Bracie told her.

Shanelle told Bracie they could go downstairs and hangout or she could take a nap. They both laughed at that thought and headed out the door. The November air was cool, but the sun was shining bright. They sat outside and talked for awhile. Bracie watched Tyler's stride as he walked to where they were sitting in the garden. 'Oh my God, he is so fine,' she thought. He sat next to Bracie and put his arm around her as they talked. Bracie moved over as if she was drawn to him. She felt comfortable in his embrace. Shanelle smiled as she saw how the two of them connected. Finally, she got up to leave the two of them alone. Tyler, being polite, told her she didn't have to leave.

Shanelle, looking at the happy couple, replied, "Oh yes I do, I'll see you this evening."

Bracie looked at Tyler.

"I invited a few friends over," he said. They sat outside to enjoy the fresh air a little while longer.

"Dress comfortably, we're eating in and hanging out inside," he told Bracie as they walked towards the house. Tyler's hand was touching her slightly in the back, and she could feel it through every stitch of clothing she had on.

Bracie

Bracie went downstairs a little past the hour, fashionably late, she thought. She followed the voices into the sitting room. All the attention turned to her when she entered the room. She had on a deep purple maxi dress with silver accessories and silver sandals. Bracie had her hair down and pulled to one side with a matching rose clip. Tyler looked at Bracie as if she were an angel. All of his friends watched as he walked over to her. They were both glowing and everyone in the room seemed happy, except Greg. He thought all women were after Tyler for his money. He looked at Tyler and knew he was too late; Tyler was already hooked on this Bracie Turner broad. Bracie mingled among Tyler's friends as if they were her own. After dinner, the men went outside. Bracie didn't know how she missed the beginning of their subject, but they were having a heated discussion on sex and love. Bracie decided she would sit this one out.

"No, having sex is not making love," Vanessa said loudly.

"Just because you are loud, don't make you right, it's all the same thing," Angela said.

"You're just saying that because that fool out there won't marry you, I don't see why you put up with his foolishness." Vanessa said to her.

Angela looked down when all the ladies said at once, "Cause I love him."

She wanted the focus off of her and so she asked Sondra, "Have you told Kenny you still don't enjoy sex or making love as you put it after two years of marriage?"

"Leave her alone," Vanessa said, "she'll grow into it."

Their conversation went on as Bracie sat and listened.

Out of the blue, Vanessa asked Bracie, "What do you think on the subject?"

Bracie told the ladies she was new to the group, and she didn't want to get involved in such an intimate discussion. Gail told Bracie she was a fresh opinion and that's what they needed. "We disagree a lot, but we still love each other."

Bracie still wasn't sure she wanted to get in on this discussion, but all eyes were on her.

"I guess I can start by telling Sondra, if you have been sexually unhappy in your marriage for two years, it's partly your fault."

Sondra looked at Bracie in shock and told her to continue because she wanted to know how this was her fault.

Bracie looked at her and said, "Because you are leading him to believe you are enjoying whatever he is or is not doing."

Sondra didn't say anything; she listened because she wanted help and so far her friends had not been able to give it to her.

Bracie continued, "Sex is the most intimate aspect in marriage and if you cannot be open and honest there, you have a big problem. As women, we set the tone in our bedroom just like we do any other part of our home. When you are with your

Bracie

husband, he has a right to know if what he is or is not doing is pleasing you. It's also important how you tell him. If he's going to the right, just tell him in an intimate sexy way to go to the left, and if that pleases you, let him know it. If you want him to kiss, explore, touch whatever you desire, tell him. Your husband loves you, and he wants to please you, but there is one thing he is not and that's a mind reader."

All the ladies looked at Bracie when Sondra asked "Won't he be angry?"

"He might be upset at first, because for two years you have kept him in the dark on how you have been feeling," Bracie answered.

Vanessa broke in again and asked, "So what's your view on making love and having sex?"

Bracie asked herself, 'Is this woman always this loud?' and then answered her question.

"This is only my opinion; same act, two different emotions. I believe you cannot truly make love to a man you are not married to. Have good sex, yes; but make love, no."

"And why is that?" asked Gail who is usually the quiet one of the group.

"Marriage gives you the freedom to give your all to your husband. When you are not married you tend to hold back, just in case. Once you are married you are free to surrender your heart, your love, and your body to your husband. Then and only then, can God bless your coming together."

Gail spoke up again and asked Bracie "So God blesses sex?"

She smiled at her and told her, "Yes, I believe he does, when you are married. God instituted sex for marriage and it's always in our best interest to wait."

Angela, feeling picked on, said rather rudely, "Well aren't you the hypocrite. You talking this good game about God and what he expects, while you are screwing Tyler!"

Everyone looked at her, shocked that she would say something of that magnitude. Bracie got up from her chair and walked over to her.

"First, I wasn't talking about you because I don't know you. Second I have not slept with Tyler. I love him, but he is not my husband, and third, if you are offended I'm sorry, but I won't apologize for the truth." Bracie told the ladies "If I have offended anyone else, I'm sorry, but you asked me into this discussion. Now if you don't mind, I will be excused."

Shanelle, Vanessa, and Gail said in unison, "Don't go, we want you to stay!"

Sondra didn't say anything, for she was thinking about what Bracie said earlier.

Vanessa said in her loud, silly voice, "So you love Tyler huh?"

Bracie turned to look at her and asked, "Where did that come from?"

All the ladies said at once, "You just said it!"

Bracie laughed and denied it.

Bracie

Vanessa teased her by repeating what she said just as she said it. Bracie didn't deny it anymore, she simply said, "Oh well," and changed the subject to Thanksgiving. This time everyone enjoyed the conversation of food, family, and fun.

Meanwhile, Tyler and the men were outside having their own heated discussion. They were discussing sports when Greg asked about Bracie.

"She's pretty and seems really nice," Josh said. Kenneth and Larry agreed.

"You seem to be happy Tyler, and it's about time."

"I am," he answered back.

"What does she want from you?" Greg asked.

"Let it rest man," all the other guys said. Tyler looked at Greg and shook his head.

"She seems nice now because she has nothing, and she knows you can give her everything," he said.

Larry told Greg to shut up. "You act like Tyler is a child. He has a right to be happy."

Greg retaliated. "He wanted to be happy when that last fool tried to claim that her child belonged to him."

They were all shocked and couldn't believe Greg would bring that up, because Tyler was hurt when the DNA results proved the little girl was not his.

Kenneth and Josh told him "That was not called for. Everyone makes mistakes, and they still deserve a chance at being happy."

Before anyone could say anything else, Tyler stood up and said "I AM right here, and I need you all to know, Bracie is my choice for now, subject closed!"

They went back to their discussion on sports, but his mind was on Bracie. After awhile, the men went back into the room where the ladies were still on the topic of food and family.

Tyler and Bracie bid each couple good night at the door. Bracie smiled when Vanessa told her on the way out of the door, "You look good right there. We'll pick you up in the morning. Be ready, and have comfortable shoes on."

Tyler and Bracie sat at the bar in the kitchen, after he finally got everyone off.

"I guess all went well since you all are hanging out tomorrow."

"Yeah, it was good," she smiled.

Bracie didn't want to bother Tyler about the exchange between her and Angela. "We are going shopping and having lunch."

Tyler could see Bracie had something on her mind. He lifted her chin and asked what was wrong.

"Do you have an idea of where we are going? I'm not broke, but I can't afford to splurge either."

Bracie

Tyler reached into his pocket and pulled out his wallet. He gave Bracie six one hundred dollar bills. She pulled her hand back as if he had shocked her.

"I'll be ok," Bracie said. Tyler moved her hand from behind her back and held it.

"Take it, please. I need to know you are going to be all right while you are out tomorrow." The tone in his voice made her accept his gift.

Tyler smiled. "All I need now is a glass of your crafty Kool-Aid," he said trying to lighten the mood.

"Hold on," Bracie said on her way up the stairs. Tyler looked and saw she left the money on the counter. He reached back into his wallet and took out four more bills and slid them in with the rest. He had already talked to Shanelle and Vanessa to find out where they would be taking her. Bracie came downstairs with a small bag in her hand. She asked Tyler for a pitcher and the sugar. She got two lemons out of the fridge and a few minutes later they were enjoying Tyler's favorite drink. They talked on for a while and Tyler walked around the bar to hug Bracie. He held her for a long moment and kissed her on the forehead and then softly on the lips.

"I'll see you in the morning." He picked the money up, folded it, and put it in her hand. He kissed her again and left her standing there and went upstairs. Tyler closed his door and went to take a cold shower.

Shanelle, Vanessa, and Bracie left the house while Tyler stood in the doorway. He wanted to kiss Bracie last night, but after he had given her the money, the timing would have been all wrong. He did not want to give her the impression of being bought. She would have walked back to Houston. He laughed at the thought. Tyler realized she was genuine and a woman of her word. Her simple and honest way of life was like a breath of fresh air. He knew he liked Bracie from their first dinner at her home and the fact that she could cook and loved to do it was an added bonus. Not having to go to restaurants all the time was a plus, also. Bracie didn't like the limelight and that made him happiest of all. That's when Tyler realized it was all about him and not the famous Tyler Shaw title. He walked to the bar and wondered how far would this relationship with Bracie Turner go? He also knew it was more than just spending time with her that was making him happy; it was Bracie herself that made him happy. Bracie didn't know it, but she had Tyler reflecting on the man he was back in New Orleans, simple and carefree, and he liked it like that.

Vanessa, Bracie, and Shanelle met up with Sondra and Gail at a local eatery for brunch. They ordered and noticed how happy Sondra was, and that she had begun to talk a mile a minute.

"Hey, slow down girl, what's up with you?" Vanessa asked in her usual loud but friendly tone.

Sondra looked at Bracie and said, "It worked! I did what you said and it worked. For the first time, Kenny and I made love, and we both enjoyed it."

"That's wonderful," Bracie said feeling very happy for her.

Sondra and the other ladies looked at Bracie and asked "You don't want details?"

Bracie looked at Sondra and the other ladies and told them, "You are married, and what goes on in your bedroom is personal and none of my business."

"But you helped me." Sondra replied.

"I told you truth. I gave you universal facts to help get you in the right direction; the ride will always be how you make it."

They looked at Bracie and for once Vanessa was speechless. When everyone finished their meal, they made a list of each store they wanted Bracie to see, and they were on their way.

Angela met them in front of The French Bistro and gave each lady a hug. They laughed and talked while listening to Bracie talk about her family and friends, especially her grandchildren. They went into Jana's Boutique to show Bracie some of her suits. Jana came out to speak to the ladies. They had been shopping here a long time and had become friends years ago.

Vanessa got everyone's attention "Hey, we do have company with us today!" She introduced Bracie as Tyler's friend. "She sings at her church, so let's try a few of your Sunday suits on her."

Jana took Bracie to the back and that began their afternoon of trying on clothes. Bracie put on a navy and white suit and fell in love with it the moment she stepped into the mirror. Jana put that suit to the side as Bracie tried on several more suits. She chose a brown and blue suit, also. Bracie wanted the two suits, but feared they would be out of her price range. She had already seen tags ranging from $500 to $1,300.

"How much are these? I looked for a tag, but I didn't see one on either suit."

Jana walked away and came back with tags in her hand. They are from my clearance rack and they are priced at $245 each. Bracie told Jana she would take the two suits and asked if she had any pantsuits around the same price. Jana left and came back with three suits for Bracie to try on. She chose a black and cream double breasted suit with shoes to match. They were headed out of the door when Bracie heard Jana tell Vanessa to tell Tyler "She is a keeper." Vanessa laughed and told her she would relay the message.

They laughed and joked around as they visited shop after shop. They were enjoying themselves when they realized Bracie had stopped in front of a jewelry store window. In it was a platinum letter T with a single diamond in it. She looked at the necklace and knew she had to get it for Tyler. The price tag was

Bracie

$3,400. She had it in her account, but it was still a lot for her. The ladies were now standing next to her looking at it. It is beautiful they agreed, but all said she shouldn't over do it.

"I want to get this for Tyler for Christmas," Bracie said, "Please don't tell him!"

"We won't, because you are not buying it," Vanessa said firmly.

Bracie saw Shanelle come out of the store and asked her if they had any of the necklaces inside. She nodded yes and Sondra elbowed her in the side. They walked inside the store and a salesman greeted them.

"May I help you ladies?"

Bracie told him she needed the letter T that was in the window. The salesman smiled at her and said they were about to reduce the price of the necklace to $2,000. She took out her bank card and I.D. and gave it to him. When the salesman gave her the box, she held it to her chest and smiled. She put her card and I.D. in her purse and headed towards the door. On the way out a sapphire and diamond bracelet caught her attention. It was dainty and cute, but had an $800 price tag.

"If you put the necklace back, you can get that for yourself." Vanessa told her.

Bracie looked at her and said "No, I would rather keep the gift for Tyler. We better head back so we can get ready for dinner."

She was in her own world so she never noticed the ladies had their own conversation going on.

Shanelle and Bracie rode back to the house in silence. She could see Bracie holding on to Tyler's box. She'd had to talk fast to get the salesman to let her pay the other $1,400 before Bracie came into the store. Tyler had told her and Vanessa not to let Bracie pay for anything with her cards. No one ever thought she would be buying something for him. She paid for the suits, shoes, and other few items with cash, so they thought she was through shopping.

"How did it go?" Tyler asked, as they walked into the house.

Bracie put the small box in her pocket and said, "Everything was fine."

Tyler saw her put the box away and looked at Shanelle.

"I'm going into the kitchen and then upstairs to shower and change," Shanelle said while walking away. Tyler picked up Bracie's bags and followed her to her room. The room smelled like her flower scent. He took a deep breath as he put her things on the bed and stepped close to her.

"Can you be ready for seven?" he asked. Bracie only nodded; she couldn't talk because he was so close to her. Tyler touched her face with the back of his fingers. She looked at him as he lifted her head and bent down to kiss her. By the time his lips touched hers, Shanelle called out her name. She knew she

Bracie

had interrupted something as soon as she stepped inside Bracie's opened door.

"See you at seven," Tyler said and walked past Shanelle agitated.

She apologized over and over.

"It's ok," Bracie assured her and tried to find out what she wanted in the first place. Shanelle told her to wear the black and cream outfit she just bought. It will be perfect for the evening. She left so Bracie could shower and change. She was probably as excited as Tyler was to see the dressier side of Bracie.

At five minutes before the time Tyler told her to be downstairs, Bracie met Tyler and Shanelle in the sitting room. She wore her hair down and full all over. Her makeup was light and just enough to let her true beauty shine through. She accessorized her outfit with a pearl necklace and matching earrings. Both Tyler and Shanelle were speechless for a moment. He stood and walked over to her.

"You look beautiful," he said.

"Thank you," she replied and took his arm.

They took the limo to the restaurant. They pulled up and Carl opened the door for Tyler. Tyler got out first, and helped Shanelle out, and then Bracie. He took her arm in his, and they met the others inside. They were seated without Sondra and Kenny. They made small talk while waiting for the other couple.

Everyone looked at Bracie when she ordered ginger ale served in a wine glass.

"I prefer not to drink," she said. Greg and Angela looked at her, but for different reasons. They had their disagreement about Bracie earlier. Greg wanted her out of the way. He was next in line for T. Wahs Production Studio, and he didn't want to share it with anyone else. He already knew that the bulk of the Productions and its holding were going to Shanelle. Tyler didn't have a wife or an heir, and Greg wanted to keep it that way. Angela knew Bracie was good for Tyler, and she told that to Greg. She tried to explain that his perception of Bracie was wrong. She loved Tyler, the man; not the stuff, not the money. She was beginning to understand now why Greg would not marry her and made her have two abortions, saying they were not ready to become parents. Bracie opened her eyes last night to some things she already knew, and she had not felt the same about Greg since.

Sondra and Kenneth arrived and took their seats right before the waiter came to take their food order. They were beaming like teenagers. Tyler caught the exchange between her and Bracie.

"Thank you," Sondra mouthed to her, Bracie nodded once and smiled. Dinner went rather well. Gail complimented Bracie on how beautiful she looked. Everyone agreed, even Greg admitted she looked nice. They ate, then enjoyed each other's

Bracie

company. The band was playing soft jazz. Tyler stood and took Bracie's hand.

"Come dance with me," he said. Bracie took his outstretched hand and went with him to the dance floor. The music was slow, so Tyler got a chance to hold her, and he liked the way Bracie felt in his arms. She enjoyed the warmth and strength of being in his embrace. The band finished the song, and the couple didn't seem to notice; they seemed to be hearing their own song. It was evident they had not realized the band stopped playing, so they began playing another number. Once again, everyone was happy, except Greg. Tyler and Bracie walked back to the table, glowing and feeling free.

On the drive home Tyler didn't know what to do next. He surely didn't want to offend her by asking her to join him in his room or vice versa. Once in the house he walked her to her room, kissed her softly at the door and told her what time to be downstairs in the morning. Tonight they would both take cold showers.

Chapter Nine

Bracie sat in her favorite chair, replaying the weekend with Tyler over and over in her head. She felt guilty, because she wanted to make love to him. Then she realized making love with him might not happen. She had to get her emotions under control. She knew Tyler cared for her, but to what extent? She had fallen in love, and it caught her off guard.

"Lord what have I done? I've given my heart to a man who may not even want it. Lord, please help me. Guide me in this relationship. Father I have fallen in love with Tyler Shaw. We are from the same background, but we live two completely different lifestyles."

Bracie said, "Amen," and got up from her chair. She really was confused, yet she knew she did not want to turn back. She had to get her focus on her poetry, because she had to be in Dallas for Saturday morning. She went over her list of poetry to decide which two she would take with her. After hours of searching and reading, she chose "My Destiny" and "Love Is Like."

Bracie walked into the Dallas Convention Center with her family.

"Calm down," Anthany said, for she was nervous and it showed. Bracie walked backstage as her family went to be seated. When the announcer called her name, Bracie walked onto the stage and quoted her poem. She finished, took a bow, and walked behind the curtain. Everyone clapped, and her family clapped for what seemed like forever. When the last person finished, the announcer called all twenty contestants to the stage. From this twenty, five will be chosen to move to the final round to compete for the grand prize. He asked for an envelope and began to call names. Bracie's name was called third and she stepped forward. After the five names were called, the announcer told them final judging would begin in one hour.

The contestants left the stage to greet their families. Bracie hugged her family and told them she was too nervous to eat. They could eat after everything was over. Trevion, Le'Andre, and Monique encouraged their grandmother by giving her a small picture with the four of them on it.

"You can do it," they told her as she walked over to where the other finalists were standing.

Five chairs were placed in the middle of the stage. The contestants had to recite their poems in the order their names had been called. Bracie was so nervous her hands were sweating. When Bracie's name was called, she stood, said another prayer, and looked at her picture. She walked to the microphone and closed her eyes. She took a deep breath and with tears in her eyes, she quoted her poem "Love is Like" from memory. When Bracie finished, she got a standing ovation. She took a bow and went back to her seat. She had written the poem for Tyler, and he was not here to hear her recite it. She smiled at her mom in the crowd and knew Ms. Deanie's single nod meant she did well. Her mom had always supported her and having her here today gave Bracie the boost of confidence that she needed. All five constants were now standing in the middle of the stage waiting for the top three places to be called. The announcer called the third place winner. When he said 'in second place,' everyone held their breath...... "Bracie Turner." Her family stood and cheered for her. After they called the first place winner, all of the contestants hugged and congratulated each other. Bracie walked off stage with a trophy and a check for $2,500.

Bracie was standing with her family when Carl walked up with a bouquet of red roses. Everyone stopped when she hugged him and accepted the roses.

"Where is Tyler, is he here?" She looked around for him.

Carl told Bracie, "He's been here since this morning. He stood in the back while you recited your poetry. He didn't want to distract you or draw any attention to himself."

"Tell him, thank you," she said with a smile.

Bracie

Anthany, Joe'Al, Raymond, and Andre' walked up and introduced themselves to Carl. He shook each of their hands as Bracie introduced him to her family. D'john and Romesha were laughing at the men grilling Carl.

"He's cute," they told Bracie.

She just laughed and said, "Thanks."

Carl finally walked over and told Bracie it was time for him to go. She hugged him again and he left. Bracie went back to her family as the ladies admired her roses.

They were leaving the Center when Carl called Bracie's name.

"Excuse me," she told her family as she went over to where he stood. He handed her a box and a card and told her, "Tyler says "Happy Birthday."

Bracie looked for the blue Audi and didn't see it.

"He wants you to open it now," and took a small step to the side which Bracie did not notice. She opened the box and stared at the bracelet.

"It's the bracelet I saw at the shop," she said choked up.

"Tell him thank you, it's beautiful, I…I," she became speechless.

Raymond walked over and asked if everything was ok. Bracie nodded as she took a rose out of the bouquet. She hugged Carl and whispered in his ear,

"This hug and rose are for Tyler." He smiled and went to a brown Bentley parked a few steps away. She looked back as Carl got into the car and saw Tyler smile and wave at her. Bracie smiled back and turned to go with her family. They went to eat and celebrate, and then headed home.

The drive back to Houston seemed like it took longer than usual. It was late when Bracie walked into her apartment. She put the trophy on the table and her flowers into a vase. She turned off the light and went into her bedroom. She put the bracelet on her nightstand and went to shower.

Bracie got on her knees to pray and thank God for such a blessed day. She was happy, and she knew it was because of God's love for her. As soon as she got under her covers the phone rang.

"Tyler," she said softly.

"Hello Bracie, you were wonderful."

"Thank you," was all she could say.

Tyler broke the silence by asking if she liked her bracelet.

"It's beautiful. Shanelle told you she was in the store when I saw it," Bracie said all at once. "I am so glad you came. I didn't think you remembered," she told him.

"Of course I remembered, I wouldn't miss something so important to you," he replied. Bracie smiled, for she felt elated. Tyler told her he was on his way back to California. He would

Bracie

be tied up for at least a month, preparing for a new movie, but would call every chance he got.

"I understand, and I will be praying for you."

She wanted to say "I love you," but chose not to - over the phone wouldn't sound right.

"Tyler," she said his name softly.

"Yes Bracie?" he asked.

"I wrote the second poem for you." She continued to speak softly into the phone.

"Tyler, are you there?" she asked.

"I'm here Bracie, thank you so much. That is the first poem that has ever been written for me." Tyler was glad he was alone, because for the first time in his life he was feeling the true emotions of love. Bracie was the first person besides his grandmother that ever told him they would be praying for him, and he actually believed it. They were saying their goodbyes when Tyler thanked Bracie for his rose. They laughed and hung up.

Chapter Ten

Thanksgiving had come and gone, and life was wonderful for Bracie. She was with Sheila and Charles when Sheila gave birth to a healthy six pound, six ounce baby girl two days after Thanksgiving. They had the glow of all first time parents. Bracie was so happy for them for she knew this would be a day they would never forget. They all took plenty of pictures with the new baby, and Bracie left so they could begin to make memories as their new journey into parenthood began.

Bracie was Christmas shopping with D'john and her three daughters-in-law when her phone rang. She talked with Sheila for a few minutes and explained there was more than one way to burp the baby. She gave her a few pointers on the baby's bath time, also. Bracie told Sheila it was her turn to laugh, because now Sheila understood what it meant to have a camera on hand at all times. They laughed and hung up. Everyone knew Bracie loved taking pictures and always had a camera with her.

"What are you getting for Carl?" they asked Bracie.

It took her a moment to remember they all thought Carl was her male friend. They took her to the men's department to help pick out a special gift for him. Bracie's mind was on the gifts she wanted to purchase for her new friends, especially Shanelle and Vanessa.

They decided they would make the drive to South Park and eat at Hicks Barbeque. She knew her nephew Terry and his wife would be there. Bracie had not eaten at Hicks since the night Dwayne kissed her. She thought about that night for a second and her thoughts went to Tyler who she still had not formally kissed. Terry came from behind the counter when the ladies walked in. His wife waved, because she was helping customers. They talked while he took their orders. Bracie's phone rang while his wife walked over and kissed her on the cheek. She began to talk to the others so Bracie could talk on the phone. Bracie looked at the number; it was Tyler. She didn't want to say his name and she didn't want to miss the call.

So she answered, "Hello Baby… yes I'm sure…I'm with my daughters…ok…bye Baby."

They just looked at her with smiles on their faces. They were so happy that she had found someone. They loved her and they saw how she suffered from grief after Matthew had passed.

She wouldn't look at another man, yet they knew she was lonely, because she and Matthew did everything together.

"What?" she asked laughing.

"Well Tyler, you done missed out," Romesha said.

"Yeah, she done upgraded Carl to baby," Tina said.

They all laughed.

Bracie looked at the four ladies in front of her and told them, "Enough of the Tyler jokes; I get enough of that with your husbands."

They agreed as they all laughed again, including Bracie. They ate their lunch while sharing stories with Bracie about her grandchildren. They paid and each gave Terry a hug on their way out of the door.

"I love you, Auntie; I know you are praying for me," he said as he walked her to the door.

"I love you nephew, and I am very proud of you. Kiss the twins for me," she told him. "Yes ma'am, keep praying for us with this new one on the way." Terry kissed his aunt as she told him, "Always," and stepped outside.

Tyler stood at the counter in his kitchen thinking about his conversation with Bracie. Baby, he thought. He smiled at such a small word, but in this context it meant so much. He dialed Shanelle's number to see if she had picked up Bracie's gift.

"I have it here, and it is beautiful. She's going to love it," Shanelle assured him. "I followed your instructions down to the detailed wrapping."

Tyler told Shanelle he would pick the gift up on his way to the airport and thanked her for her help and they hung up. Shanelle turned to Carl and asked if he had their reservations for Christmas Eve and Christmas morning.

"Everything is taken care of," he said. He kissed her and headed out the door. Tyler felt bad about asking Carl to be away from California on Christmas Eve, but Carl assured Tyler he had plans that would keep him busy and happy while in Houston. Tyler had no idea whatsoever that Shanelle was Carl's plan. Bracie made sure she talked with Sondra, Gail, and Angela the week of Christmas because she talked with Shanelle and Vanessa more often. Vanessa had a lovely sense of humor and always made Bracie laugh. Her friendship with Shanelle had become solid for she knew Bracie loved Tyler and meant well for him.

It was Christmas Eve, and everyone was having lunch at Raymond and Tiffany's home. Bracie's grandchildren seem to be everywhere. JeKeith walked up to Bracie, put his fingers to her lips, and smiled.

"Grandma," she said several times.

He moved his mouth and made his regular sounds. Bracie knew it was just a matter of time before he would say grandma. He would not give up, and she wouldn't let him. She kissed his forehead, and he went to find something to get into with the other children. Bracie looked at her watch and knew she had to leave soon. She had not seen Tyler since Dallas last month and had not spent quality time with him since the week before that. She wanted everything to be perfect. She hoped this would be the first of many Christmases together for them. Everyone decided to spend Christmas at their own homes and they would all exchange gifts at Ms. Deanie's during Sunday dinner.

Bracie's children turned her way.

Anthany spoke out first, "Mama is spending Christmas day with us."

Before she could say anything D'john said, "She can come home and spend Christmas Eve with us, and ride over to Anthany's with us."

Joe'Al and Raymond agreed she could stay where she wanted, but she would not be spending Christmas Eve alone this year.

Bracie stood and told them all, "I am spending Christmas Eve at my own home, and I can drive myself to Anthany's around noon. And y'all please don't show up at my house, because I will not open the door." They all laughed as if they never gave that a thought.

"Let me have my time; I need it, and I promise I am okay." They all agreed not to show up unannounced. Anthany wanted to go over anyway, but Joe'Al advised them all to leave her

Bracie

alone. Joe'Al looked at Anthany who at this point somehow believed he was their father and not just their eldest brother.

Bracie checked to make sure everything was in order for Tyler's visit. He would be staying overnight and she really didn't know what to expect. She remembered the look on his face when she told him she was celibate and had not been with a man since Matthew passed two and a half years ago. Tyler knew she meant it when she said sex before marriage was never an option. Bracie was shocked, but very glad when he called her again after that conversation. Now she hoped he had taken her seriously. She sat in her favorite chair and leaned her head back. Bracie didn't realize she dozed off until she heard the knock at the door. She opened it and Tyler stood there with two bags and two dozen red and pink roses.

"Come in out of the cold," she said. Tyler put one foot in and gave Bracie the roses and the small bag. The other he sat inside near the door. She looked at him when he bent down outside the door and picked up a beautifully wrapped box. He came in and closed the door with his foot. He walked over and put the box under the tree while Bracie locked the door. Tyler stood back and admired her tree.

"It's beautiful," he said.

"Thank you, I decorated it myself." Bracie smiled. She sat the bouquet on the table by her chair as usual. They sat down and caught up on the events of the last month.

The timer on the stove went off, and Bracie went into the kitchen. Tyler followed and offered to help. She poured the water off of the angel hair pasta and put the pot back on the stove. She sliced red and yellow bell peppers, while Tyler sliced tomatoes and cumbers for the salad. After Bracie mixed the pasta, peppers, and sauce together she served it on blue china plates with grilled shrimp on top. Tyler put salad on separate plates and put them on the table also. He lit the candles while Bracie placed the wine glasses on the table.

"I have white wine," she said.

Tyler nodded and she poured him a full glass and herself half a glass. The lights from the tree and the candles gave the room a very romantic ambiance. Bracie turned the stereo on and put in her favorite jazz Christmas CD. She took the breadsticks out of the oven and put them in the middle of the table. Tyler could not keep his eyes off of Bracie. *I wonder if she realizes how beautiful she is,* he thought. Bracie looked up to find him staring at her. She blushed, and he laughed.

"What?" she asked.

"It's good to see someone really blush," he smiled at her.

Breaking the ice, they began talking about the Christmas holiday in general.

"It's my favorite time of year. Everyone seems to be happy when they know the true meaning of Christmas."

Tyler leaned back in his chair and told Bracie, "Your meal was excellent."

Bracie

"Why thank you. Would you like a slice of Key Lime pie?"

"I can't eat another bite right now, but maybe later," he said.

Tyler and Bracie went into the living room to relax. Tyler sat on the sofa, while Bracie pulled out four Christmas movies and gave them to Tyler.

"Put them in the order you would like to see them."

"Ok," he said.

Bracie laughed when he chose the old classic, Rudolph the Red Nosed Reindeer; it was one of her favorites. She put the movie in and went back to sit in her chair.

"Ump," Tyler cleared his throat to get her attention. "Come sit here," he said patting the sofa next to him.

Bracie sat next to Tyler, and he put his arm around her and pulled her close to him. Bracie snuggled under Tyler and they watched the movie. When Bracie got up to change the movie, Tyler asked for the restroom. While he was out of the room Bracie got out a blanket and put it on the sofa. She went into the kitchen and took out two cups and mix for hot chocolate. As she put the milk on the stove, Tyler walked in to help.

"Wow, the temperature sure has dropped," he said. Bracie agreed, as they snuggled on the sofa. She was sleepy after two movies. When she yawned a third time, Tyler said it was time for bed.

Bracie told Tyler she would be first in the shower and to make himself at home. He looked around and pulled out one of her scrapbooks. He admired her love for her family. He laughed at some of the captions on the pictures. Bracie came out in a blue pajama set and stood in the door way. He knew then she didn't realize how beautiful and sexy she was inside and out. Tyler picked up his overnight bag and went into her room. He noticed their picture on the side of her bed. It was one they had taken on the beach in the Bahamas. Bracie gave Tyler a bag and said, "I hope they fit."

He opened the bag and took out a pair of navy pajamas. He looked at the tag and said they should fit fine. Tyler took his bag and went into the restroom. Bracie closed the door to her bedroom so he could have some privacy.

While Tyler was in the back, Bracie inflated and made up her guest bed in front of the tree. She took out the extra pillows she had set aside for him. She removed the movie and put in her yuletide DVD. She gathered the cups and went back into the kitchen. Bracie turned to see Tyler standing there watching her as she began to clean up.

"Well I think I should help since I enjoyed some of that great cooking," he said.

"You don't have too."

"I know I don't, but I want to," he said walking into the kitchen.

He noticed her wine glass was still the same minus the two sips she had during dinner. Bracie washed while Tyler rinsed and

Bracie

dried. She put the pasta that was left into a bowl. She snapped the lid and opened the fridge.

"Is that my crafty Kool-Aid?" Tyler asked.

Bracie laughed and took it out. "You get the glasses and I'll pour," she said.

They took the glasses into the living room. They didn't talk much; they enjoyed the music and the fireplace. The lights on the tree danced around the walls of the room. Bracie yawned again, and Tyler told her it was time to turn it in. She got up and went into her room. She left the door half opened in case Tyler needed something. She got on her knees to pray. Tyler stood to put the blanket on the bed and saw Bracie on her knees. He wanted to watch her, but didn't want to intrude on her time with the Father. When she finished praying, Bracie realized she left everything on in the front. Tyler was lying on his stomach looking at the lights and decorations on the tree. Bracie stood and watched him before she got his attention.

"I forgot to ask if you want me to turn off the tree and/or the television?"

Tyler looked at Bracie and shocked her once again.

"You can leave them both on if you will come and enjoy them with me," he said.

She stood there not knowing what to do or say. Tyler sat up and pulled the covers back on the bed.

He looked into her eyes and told her, "I understand your beliefs, and I will not do anything to dishonor that, I promise."

He reached out his hand, and she took it. Bracie sat on the bed, then lay in his arms. They watched the fireplace and Tyler told her how neat it was to see a fireplace burning on DVD.

Bracie asked Tyler if he would mind if she turned off the tree; she could not sleep with the light in her face. The moment she turned the tree off, she wished she had not. The light and crackling from the fireplace made it too romantic, and romance was something she couldn't handle right now. Bracie was tired and her body started to relax. Tyler held Bracie, and her flower scent was all he could smell. Please don't, he kept telling his body, but the warmth and scent of her body made his body disobedient. Bracie could feel Tyler against her. She tensed up and tried to scoot away without him noticing. He did. Tyler pulled her closer into his arms and put her head on his chest. He kissed the top of her head.

"I promised, now go to sleep."

Bracie put her arm over his chest and released all of her tension.

"I love you, Tyler," she said, not realizing she was thinking out loud on her way to sleep. He lay there listening to her breathe, remembering her words. He didn't know how to process her unknown confession. Tyler finally dozed off, too.

Carl and Shanelle were lying in bed at the hotel downtown. Carl told her, "Tyler has fallen in love with Ms. Bracie."

Bracie

Shanelle agreed and told him, "Greg does not like Bracie. He thinks she is after Tyler's money and possessions."

"I don't trust him; he always seems to be up to no good. We have to keep a close eye on him because he's going to cause trouble," Carl said.

Shanelle kissed Carl and told him "Enough about Greg. I don't want to talk about him anymore."

Carl held her close and asked, "Do you think Tyler and Ms. Bracie will make love tonight?"

Shanelle thought about their conversation and said, "It may be hard, but I'll bet everything I have on a No!"

They laughed and turned out the lights when Carl said, "Oh well, we are."

Bracie's phone rang early the next morning.

"Hello," she answered.

"Thank you John, Merry Christmas to you too. We'll talk later."

She hung up and put her phone on silent and went back to sleep in Tyler's arms. She never noticed Tyler was already awake when her phone rang. *John, who is John?* he thought. A touch of jealousy touched at Tyler's heart. He looked at her sleeping in his arms.

"This looks perfect," he said under his breath. Bracie stirred, but only to shift positions. He let her get comfortable and closed his eyes for only a moment before he was asleep again.

Bracie stretched then moved slowly off the bed so she wouldn't wake Tyler. She went into the restroom to freshen up. She laid her clothes out for the day and went into the kitchen. The smell of coffee woke Tyler up. He sat on the side of the bed and stretched. Bracie walked over to him and kissed him on the cheek.

"Good morning, sleepy head. Merry Christmas. I put your face towels in the bathroom already."

"Merry Christmas to you, Bracie," He stuck his feet into his slippers and went into the bathroom. Bracie had pancake mix made, sausage and bacon already cooked, and she was about to crack the eggs when Tyler said, "I got the eggs." She stepped over to the griddle and made pancakes while he scrambled the eggs. They sat the food on the table ,and Bracie poured two cups of coffee. They were eating when he finally realized he had not bought slippers with him. When he mentioned it, Bracie laughed.

"Yeah, I bought them when I got your pajamas. I got your shoe size from a pair of your sandals. I hope you slept well," she said.

"Like a baby," was his reply.

Tyler went to the tree and got a small bag and gave it to Bracie. She took a box out of the bag and opened it.

Bracie

"It's beautiful," she said as she took the angel with diamond and sapphire wings out of the box. Tyler walked around her to snap the pendant around her neck. She stood and kissed him quickly on the lips. She reached over to the counter.

"For you," she said and gave him his box.

Tyler remembered her sticking the box in her pocket. He opened it and looked at the necklace; he was speechless. He knew she sacrificed a lot to get it for him. He stood up again and took her in his arms.

"Let me put it on you," she said to get out of his grip. "I've never seen you wear jewelry, but I could not pass it up," she told him.

"I'm glad you didn't," he replied.

"We need to move the bed so you can open your box."

They let the bed down and folded the linen, then set everything on the counter. Tyler sat Bracie on the sofa and put the box on the table in front of her.

"Wait!" She got her camera and took pictures of the beautiful box before she opened it. She noticed the bow had her name on it with roses flowing down the ribbon. She looked over at Tyler and smiled.

"Give me the camera and open the box," he said.

Bracie pulled the bow and paper off. She opened the top and looked down at the prettiest black baby doll she had ever seen. She looked up at Tyler with tears streaming down her face. He put the camera down and walked over to the box. He reached in and took the doll out as if she were a baby.

He smiled at Bracie and said, "A baby for my baby."

Bracie took the doll and hugged Tyler about as tightly as he had hugged her earlier. He got the camera and took pictures as she held the doll and inspected it like a mom would her new baby. Bracie looked at the beautiful pink and white outfit the doll had on. She smiled at Tyler when she saw the roses on the border of the doll's dress. She had on matching pink booties with white lace socks. Then Bracie noticed the detailed work done on the pink blanket. Where the blanket folded back her name was embroidered surrounded by roses. She had tears in her eyes again. She could barely speak when she tried to thank him again. Tyler stopped taking pictures to watch her with the doll. Here before him was the truest form of gratitude he had ever seen. His gift touched her heart and her gratitude touched his.

"We better get dressed; I am expecting Carl at noon," Tyler said.

"You can use the bedroom first," Bracie told him.

Tyler got his garment bag out of the front closet and went into Bracie's room. He stood at the foot of her bed and imagined himself making love to her there. Oh God, he realized his thoughts caused him to get in trouble. Getting dressed took a little longer because he surely was not going out like this.

Bracie

Meanwhile Bracie sat there touching her necklace and looking at her doll. He listened, and he'd heard her. He got her exactly what she had been wanting for so many years. Tyler came out with his bag in hand. Bracie took the doll and laid her on the bed. She got dressed rather quickly, because her clothes were already laid out. She noticed his pajamas folded at the end of the bed and asked him about them.

"Keep them here; you never know when I will need a place to stay for the night."

She knew what he meant and said okay.

Bracie asked Tyler to help her load her car. He took all the gifts for her family downstairs and loaded them in her trunk. They came back into the house, and Tyler leaned against one of the bar stools.

"Bracie, will you come over here please?" She got out of her chair, walked over, and stood in front of him.

"Please let me kiss you," he said. She smiled and stepped into his embrace. Tyler kissed her face and then her lips. Bracie touched the only place she felt was safe. She caressed his face and kissed him softly on the lips. She slid her hand to the back of his head and pulled him into the kiss. This is too good, she thought, as she broke the kiss and looked at Tyler. She bit her bottom lip. Tyler gently removed her lip from her mouth and kissed her deeply again.

Bracie realized she was standing between his legs. Her next step closer confirmed what they were both feeling. Bracie stepped back; she knew she should stop, but couldn't. Tyler lifted her chin and kissed her again. Bracie put one arm around his neck and with the other she caressed the back of his head. Bracie's lips danced with his. She kissed him slowly, with passion.

Oh my God, Tyler thought as he pulled her closer to him. At this very moment, he thanked God that he was so tall because he had Bracie completely wrapped in his arms. His body moved against her to the same dance as her kiss. Tyler could hear her soft moan.

Tyler's phone buzzed and startled them both. It buzzed again, and Bracie let go, but couldn't move. Tyler pulled out his phone and answered it.

"Ok," was all he said. Bracie stepped back so he could stand up. She turned so he could adjust his pants into a more comfortable position.

"Wait inside, I'll be back up," Tyler told her as he took his bags downstairs to Carl. Bracie picked up another bag for Tyler.

"What is this?" he asked.

"Gifts for my friends in California. It's not much, but I wanted to get them something," she said.

"They understand. It's the thought that counts, Bracie."

They walked onto the porch. When Tyler touched the second step, Bracie told him to hold on as she went back into the house.

Bracie

She came back with a single rose and told him "For you." He took the rose and they shared another long kiss. Carl stood at the car smiling. In thirteen years, he had never seen Tyler Shaw display any type of affection for a woman in public.

"I'll call you later," he promised as he walked down the stairs.

She nodded and turned to go inside. Bracie stopped and told Tyler, "Carl's gift is in the bag, too."

When she went into her bedroom she could smell Tyler's cologne. Bracie touched her lips; they were still tender from the kisses she shared with Tyler. Bracie knew she wanted more of Tyler, she needed more of Tyler. She loved him, but she did not know if she was ready for the passionate battle that lay ahead of her. She had to shower and change so the scent of Tyler's cologne would not be on her.

Chapter Eleven

Bracie enjoyed Christmas with her family. They had eaten and were sitting at the table when D'john and Romesha complimented her on her pendant. All four of the men looked at her.

"Wow, Mama. Carl must love you to get you a necklace like that," Andre' said.

"Stop being messy," D'john told her husband.

"Naw, naw look, this Carl knows she likes angels," he said while flapping his arms like wings. Everyone laughed at his humor except Anthany.

"When did Carl come to your house?" he asked.

Bracie shook her head, "He came by this morning, now let it go."

She played a game of cards and told her family she was ready to go home.

Bracie

"Mama, do you need one of the kids to go with you?" Anthany asked her.

Bracie told her son, "No!" and headed out the door.

Bracie sat in her chair and looked at her tree. She took another rose out of her arrangement and thought about Tyler. She'd slept in his arms last night, and it felt good. She thought about the way he held her and kissed her. He had not crossed that line and that made Bracie happy. She picked up her camera to look at the pictures they had taken. She chose one of Tyler sitting in her chair by the tree to enlarge. She would frame it and put it on her bedside table. Bracie went to her desk and turned on her computer; she had 113 messages. She had not been on the computer in over two weeks. She opened a message from Dwayne. It read, *Hello Sweetie, haven't talked to you in a while. I hope all is well with you. Tell the family I say hello. Maybe we can have lunch soon. Merry Christmas, Dwayne.* Bracie hit the reply button and wrote: *Hello Mr. B. You are right, it has been awhile since we have talked. We did promise to stay in touch so let me know when you are free for lunch or dinner. Merry Christmas, Take care, and Be Blessed, Bracie.* She hit the send button and logged out.

Bracie opened her bank statement. She looked at the balance and knew a mistake had been made somewhere. She hit the account activity button to see what was going on. There it was in black and white, deposit from Tyler Shaw $6,500. She looked at the date. He made the deposit the second week in December. She shut down her computer and picked up her phone to call Tyler, when it rang.

"Hello."

"Hey, how was the rest of your day?" he asked.

"It was good," Bracie replied. Tyler noticed right away she didn't sound happy to hear him.

"Bracie what's wrong, is everything ok?"

She didn't respond right away.

"Bracie talk to me," he said concerned.

"I just checked my bank account and it says you deposited $6,500 into it. Why would you do that without asking me, and how did you get my information?"

This time it took him a moment to respond. "When you were at the house your bank statement must have fallen out of your luggage. Cora found it when she was cleaning and gave it to me. I meant to send it to you, but misplaced it on my desk. When I found it, I wanted to be sure you were taken care of. Don't be mad at me, Bracie."

She didn't say anything right away. They were both quiet.

"Tyler?"

"Yes?" he replied.

"I'm not angry, but you could see from my balance, I'm not broke or struggling, so why?"

Bracie

"I don't know Bracie. I heard you talking about shopping, and I wanted to replace what you would spend so you wouldn't go in the hole."

He also wanted to replace what she had spent on his necklace, but would never tell her that. He was very careful about when he made that deposit so Bracie would not know that was what he was doing. Bracie told Tyler she appreciated the fact he thought about her financial well-being, but she barely spent $1,500 on Christmas this year.

"And that's fine," he said and hurried to change the subject.

"What are you doing right now?" he asked.

"I am putting your pajamas and slippers away and getting my clothes ready for church tomorrow."

"You love your church don't you?" Tyler asked.

Bracie did love her church. She joined her church when she was nine years old. It is where she first heard God's plan of salvation and the first time she was taught God loves her. For so long she wondered how her mother made it through the hell she had to endure. As a child, Bracie knew her escape was across the street at Dwayne's house, but her mom's seemed to be the church.

Bracie refocused and answered Tyler, "Yes I do love my church. Pastor and Sister Brooks not only teach us God's Word, they live it before us."

Tyler could hear the pride in her voice. He had not attended church regularly since he left New Orleans. Bracie called his name again.

"Oh, I'm sorry, what was your question?" he asked.

"Do you want a CD of tomorrow's service?"

"Please. I have really enjoyed the ones you have given me. I share them with Shanelle and Carl."

"Wonderful," Bracie said.

They talked for about an hour sharing the rest of their Christmas Day.

Tyler sat in his garden enjoying the sunshine, when Carl and Shanelle walked out to where he was sitting.

"What's up, why are you sitting out here?" they asked.

"Just relaxing and wondering what Bracie is doing at church." Tyler knew he could always talk to Carl and Shanelle; they had become like family. He asked Carl years ago to stop calling him Mr. Shaw or boss when they were not engaged in business. Tyler treated him more like a brother and friend than an employee. Both Shanelle and Carl told Tyler to thank Bracie for the lovely Christmas gifts. Tyler told them Bracie's family thought Carl was her boyfriend. He remembered her sons approaching Carl the weekend they were in Dallas. They laughed when Carl told Tyler to be careful because that oldest boy had a mama detector on Bracie somewhere. Tyler realized how loved Bracie was, and he wanted to be a part of that.

Bracie

    Church service was over, and Bracie's family was headed to Ms. Deanie's for dinner. John was outside, she slowed down enough to invite him over for dinner. By the time John made his arrival, all the children were opening gifts and the grownups were eating.

    "Hey fam!" he said as he entered the dining room with two bags in his hand. He gave one to Bracie and the other to Ms. Deanie.

    "Thank you," they both said.

    Bracie pulled out a chair for him and went to fix his plate. She sat his plate and a glass of tea in front of him. They all laughed and talked. John kept them all laughing as he talked about his crazy road trips. Everyone enjoyed dinner at her mom's house every Sunday. Bracie heard Tyler's voice and turned towards the television. When she got up and moved to hear the interview about his upcoming movie, she didn't realize John and her mother were watching her as she watched Tyler. This time she heard none of the jokes. Just as she touched the angel on her neck, Tyler touched the T on his. Bracie's smile could have lit up the room. After the interview went off, she just sat there a moment to reflect on their Christmas together. While Bracie was in her thoughts, John and Ms. Deanie were talking about what they had just seen.

    "Do you really think she is seeing him, Mama Deanie?" John asked her.

"I know she is, and she's doing all she can to keep it private," she replied. John was concerned because he didn't know if Bracie was ready for the greedy mentality of the rich and famous. He knew he could not steer her away now for she was in love with Tyler Shaw. John had not seen that look in her eyes since Matthew. He watched her as she seem to float around the room. Yeah, she is in love, he said to himself.

Bracie's phone rang and she stepped on the porch to answer it.

"Hey... We are at mama's... Yes Tyler, I saw the interview; you look so handsome... Ok, we will talk later, bye." John stood by the door getting ready to go out when he heard Bracie mention Tyler's name. He walked away for he would never invade on her private conversation. Once again he prayed and asked God to protect her heart.

Greg sat at his desk looking for some papers he could not let Tyler or Angela find. He did not want to risk the cleaning personnel finding them and showing them to Tyler either. Angela knocked on the door as she entered.

"Hello, baby," she said to him.

Greg only glanced up from his search to tell her to come on in.

"What is Tyler up to?"

Angela told him she heard he spent Christmas Eve with Bracie.

Bracie

"Well I hope he gets what he wants and stays away from her."

Before Angela could say anything Greg told her not to say a word where Bracie was concerned. He wanted Tyler away from her. He had gotten rid of the others and Tyler's last mistake was still costing him. Everybody has a price, he thought, I just have to find hers.

Angela told him once again to let Tyler choose whom he pleases. Greg told her to shut up because this was business, something she knew nothing about. Angela knew he would do anything to get his way. She turned and walked out in disgust.

'Watch Meeting' was over and the church brought in another year with everyone on their knees in prayer. Pastor Roland asked God's blessings upon the congregation for the New Year. Bracie gave as well as received a lot of hugs, kisses, and best wishes for a new year. Her children and grandchildren were all there.

"I'm going home," Bracie told her family.

Necia wanted to go with her grandmother and Bracie said it was okay. They hugged a few more members and left. Bracie put Necia down in her bed. She showered and changed into a blue gown set. She checked on Necia and went into the front.

Bracie sat in her chair and took out a single rose. She sniffed it and thought about Tyler. She sat there for a little while longer wondering what the New Year had in store for her. She got up to go to her room when someone knocked on the door. She looked at the clock, and it said 2:17am.

"Who is it?" she asked.

"Tyler!"

Bracie opened the door and let him in. He removed his coat and she stepped into his warm embrace. They went into the kitchen and sat at the table and talked. Tyler reached over and touched Bracie's hand. She smiled at his touch. Just then Necia walked into the kitchen.

"Hello," she said to Tyler, "My name is Necia, and this is my grandma."

He reached out, shook her hand, and introduced himself only as Mr. Tyler.

"What's the matter baby?" Bracie asked her granddaughter.

"I heard noises," she said.

Bracie assured her the noise she heard was her and Tyler. She took Necia back to bed. Bracie turned on the night light, kissed Necia on the head and closed the door behind her. When she went back into the front, Tyler was sitting in her chair. He got up and walked towards the door.

"You leaving already?" she asked.

"Yeah, Carl is waiting for me downstairs. I had to come see you for the New Year."

Tyler pulled Bracie into his arms and kissed her. He thought it would be a quick kiss, but he quickly found out he wanted

Bracie

more. He held her tighter as they deepened the kiss. He stepped back and looked at Bracie.

"I better go now," he leaned down and kissed her again. Tyler picked up the rose she laid on the table earlier and left out the door. She stood there wanting him to come back, but knew it was best he leave. Bracie didn't sleep too well that morning.

Church service was very good. The first Sunday of the New Year and she was torn because as much as she wanted to be with Tyler, she knew it couldn't happen. There was no one to talk to because she didn't want anyone to know about him. Bracie saw John's truck and pulled into the driveway. She called his phone and asked him to come outside. He was walking out of the door as they hung up. John got in and looked at Bracie. Behind her glow was a look of concern.

"What's the matter Bracie?" he asked her.

"I...I don't know what I'm doing any more," she told him, as tears began to stream down her face. John's next question caught her completely off guard.

"What's going on between you and Tyler Shaw?"

She looked at him and asked how he knew?

He tried to soften the mood by saying, "Because I'm John."

Bracie smiled and told John "I love him," and dropped her head.

He lifted her chin so she could look at him. "Bracie after awhile kissing is not going to be enough if you don't stop."

"I know, but this is not like the Dwayne issue," she said.

"I know that, Bracie, and that makes the temptation even greater. If you could, you would have pulled him through the television last Sunday. You were so into him, you never noticed the jokes, and they were so busy teasing, they did not notice how you were looking at him." John could tell she didn't want the lecture, but needed the advice.

He smiled, "Bracie I heard you talking to him on the phone."

She glanced up for a second.

"I always tell you it's amazing that how you feel shows on your face, and last Sunday it showed."

"I love him, John, and I don't really know how he feels about me. Sometimes I feel like I'm too old to care, but I do. I want him to love me," she said as tears filled her eyes again.

John did what Bracie had always trusted him to do, tell her the truth. "Bracie, Tyler loving you is not going to make your situation any easier. Actually saying no will become harder. Stop beating yourself up; you have to realize you are human. You want to be loved, your body wants to be touched, and you have desires that need to be filled, but you don't want the guilt and regrets."

"I know, but I want to make love to him," Bracie said as the tears rolled down her face.

"Don't cry, that doesn't make you a bad person, that is what makes you, you. I know you Bracie and I know how strong your convictions are, but sex and passion are mighty powerful tools.

Bracie

You can't play around with them. If you don't watch it, you will be in bed with Tyler. I know you love him, but you cannot give Tyler what is not yet his. Don't let your heart overrule your head. Remember, only God can keep the two in sync."

Bracie looked at John and shook her head "I can't believe I'm getting this advice at 52 years old. I should be trying to teach this to younger women."

He laughed and told her, "As long as you live and have desires, you will never be too old for good advice." John gave Bracie a hug and told her to cheer up and be careful, as he got out of the car. Once again, Bracie thanked God for her friend.

Bracie tried not to concentrate on being with Tyler, but talking to him four and five times a week was making it difficult. In frustration, Bracie picked up her phone and texted Dwayne to see when he would be free for lunch or dinner. He was glad to hear from her, and they agreed to meet the following Friday night for dinner.

Dwayne and Bracie sat down at their table. After they put in their food order they began to talk.

"What have you been doing?" he asked her.

Bracie was about to tell him about Tyler, then realized she didn't want him to know she was seeing anyone at all. Bracie told him she came in second place in the poetry contest. They talked about their families and their jobs. They talked about a lot of nothing things in general. When the waiter came to ask Dwayne about his order, Bracie drifted back to their childhood.

Dwayne stood on his steps waiting for her to come across the street. He didn't want to play on the porch, he wanted to run and have fun. They would crawl over the wall of his porch and play hide and seek. She would let him catch her, because she liked the idea of him chasing and then catching her. With the catch there always came a hug. Bracie remembered playing on their Whirly Bird. That was her airplane, she laughed to herself. They would pump it so it would go very fast. Bracie felt free, as the Whirly Bird went around and around.

"A penny for your thoughts?" Dwayne said to get her attention.
"They are worth more than that," Bracie laughed.
She shared her thoughts about the Whirly Bird and they both laughed.
"I forgot about that," he said. "I bet if I sat on one now it would pop a wheelie."
They both laughed at his humor.
"Those were the days," he said.
If only you knew Bracie thought to herself. They enjoyed dinner and promised again to stay in touch.

Chapter Twelve

Tyler hung up from talking with Bracie. She would meet him in Austin on Friday. Tyler sat at his desk wondering what steps he wanted to take in their relationship, for he had been seeing her for over seven months now. Tyler knew he could not stop thinking about her. He wanted to be a part of her life, but how much of a part, he did not know. This weekend would help him decide. He didn't have anything specific planned; he needed to weigh out his options, then thought - what options?

Carl picked Bracie up early that afternoon. They talked most of the way to Austin. By the time Carl drove up in front of the hotel, he knew why Tyler and Shanelle were so crazy about her.

Tyler and Shanelle greeted them in the lobby. He kissed Bracie and took her bags. Tyler asked Carl to join them for dinner and turned towards the elevators. Tyler and Bracie had a suite while Shanelle chose to have her own room on a lower floor. Tyler showed Bracie the room she would be using for the weekend.

"My bedroom is next door." He pointed.

She smiled and said ok.

"We will meet Shanelle and Carl downstairs at 7:30 p.m."

Bracie went into the room and sat on the bed. She lay back and dozed off to sleep. Tyler's knock woke Bracie up.

"I'll be out in a minute," she said hurrying into the bathroom.

Bracie couldn't believe she showered, dressed, did her hair and makeup in less than thirty minutes. Before Tyler could knock on the door again, Bracie stepped out in a navy blue pantsuit with a charcoal colored blouse and shoes. Tyler and Bracie left to meet Carl and Shanelle in the dining room. They had a wonderful dinner and were enjoying the music when Greg and Angela walked up.

"Dang," Shanelle said loud enough for the other three to hear.

Tyler stood and spoke to Greg and gave Angela a hug.

"Hi. I didn't expect to see you until tomorrow morning," Tyler said.

Greg looked at Bracie and said, "I'm sure!" Tyler overlooked the remark.

"We have eaten already, but you are welcomed to join us for cocktails," he said.

Bracie

"No thank you," Greg said as he looked down his nose at Carl.

Bracie saw the look, and she also saw Carl squeeze Shanelle's hand.

"It's okay," he whispered to her.

Bracie smiled at Angela and spoke to her.

"Hello Bracie," was all she said and turned her head.

Greg took her by the elbow and they walked off. By the time Tyler sat down Carl had gotten Shanelle to calm down.

"He has a serious problem," Tyler said.

"More serious than you know," Shanelle replied.

Carl changed the subject and put everyone back into a mellow mood.

Tyler looked at his watch and stood up. He pulled out Bracie's chair for her to get up.

"It's almost midnight. We are going up. Shanelle I'll see you tomorrow morning at eight in the Golden East Conference Room.

She bid the couple good night and turned her attention to Carl.

Once inside their suite, Tyler walked Bracie to her bedroom door and kissed her. Bracie held on to his arms as she kissed him back. Tyler stepped back and opened her door.

"I'll see you after the meeting. Sleep in if you like."

Bracie nodded and went into her room. Tyler reached in and closed the door. He went into his room and took another cold shower. Tyler lay in bed thinking about Bracie being in the next room. He had lost count of how many cold showers he had taken since their first kiss.

"What has she done to me?" he kept asking himself. He never answered back because he really could not explain it.

Bracie was up and downstairs around midmorning. She saw Carl in the front lobby.

"Wanna have brunch?" he asked.

Bracie said yes, and off they went.

Tyler's movie required on-site footage in Austin; getting permission and mapping out the final details were taking longer than expected. The meeting was finally over after five. The six of them met for dinner in the hotel's dining room. After dinner the men excused themselves from the table so the ladies had a few moments alone. Bracie was glad they got a chance to talk to Angela. She apologized to Shanelle and Bracie for not being able to join them on the previous night. Angela tried to apologize for Greg's rude behavior, but both ladies agreed it was him, and it was not her fault. The men returned, but Tyler did not sit down.

"If you all would excuse us, we will be calling it a night."

Bracie

Bracie stood and bid the ladies goodnight and left with Tyler. Greg shook his head in disgust and got up.

"Come on Angela, let's go," he said without acknowledging Carl or Shanelle.

They sat and enjoyed the music a little while longer and decided they would go to their room also.

It was after midnight, and Bracie still could not sleep. She got up, put on her robe, and went into the kitchenette to get something to drink. Tyler heard her moving around and got up.

"Are you ok?" he asked.

Bracie said yes, and walked over to the floor length windows. She looked out over Austin and admired its beauty at night. Tyler walked up behind her and took her in his arms. Bracie stepped back and relaxed in his embrace. They both stood there looking out of the window. By the time Bracie figured she should move and go back to her room it was too late. Tyler kissed her on the back of her neck. Bracie turned and kissed him. She looked at Tyler as he led her over to the sofa. Tyler sat Bracie down and got on his knees in front of her. He leaned her back on the sofa pillows and kissed her again. Tyler let go of her lips and kissed her neck. Bracie caressed the back of his head while his lips teased at her neck and ears. Tyler took his time so he could make a mental note of what she liked. When he got to the base of her neck, Bracie's grip tighten around him, and she whispered his name. When Bracie said his name again, it took all he had to stay in control. She kissed Tyler's face slowly and teased his ears with her hands. Tyler was kneeling in front of her and Bracie could feel him pressing against her through her gown. When Bracie started to move her hips, Tyler pulled her closer to him. Tyler reached up to kiss her again while he pushed her gown off her shoulders. Bracie's low moan was getting the best of him, but he knew he could not, he would not rush this. Tyler ran his lips back down her neck and this time he knew where to go.

"Oh Tyler," Bracie whispered as he kissed her bare skin. He kissed her throat as he continued to tease her body. Bracie moaned his name in a way he had never heard it before. He needed her now. Tyler lifted her chin and looked into her eyes.

"Let me make love to you, Bracie," he said.

Tyler's voice brought her back. Before Bracie could say a word tears were falling down her face. She looked at her gown pushed down to her waist and the shame she felt showed on her face. She pulled it up to cover her exposed breast and felt even more ashamed when she saw that her body stood out from his touch.

Bracie looked at Tyler, crying and said "I can't, I want to, but I can't." She shook her head and whispered "I'm sorry, I'm so sorry, Tyler. I should not have let this happen." She maneuvered her legs and got up. Bracie looked at Tyler and dropped her head.

Bracie

She turned and Tyler caught her arm, "Bracie don't walk away, it's okay."

She felt so ashamed, she wouldn't look at him anymore. Bracie held on to her gown and went into her room. She lay in her bed and cried until she finally fell asleep. Tyler lay in his bed listening to her cry. He wanted to go in and comfort her, but decided against it. He could not get Bracie's look of hurt and shame out of his mind. Tyler listened as tears ran down his face, too.

Bracie cried until her eyes were red and swollen. The next morning, Tyler looked at her standing by the door and told her to sit down. He called the gift shop and ordered a pair of shades for her. She still would not look at him.

Bracie's trip home was quiet; she sat in the back like a child who had been disciplined. Carl noticed right away that something was wrong. Bracie had on shades, but he could tell she had been crying. Bracie not asking about Shanelle was another sign that something was not right. Carl tried to make small talk with Tyler on the way, but failed. When they pulled up to Bracie's apartment, Tyler told Carl he could take care of it. He got Bracie's bag out of the trunk and walked her upstairs. When she kept fumbling with the keys, Tyler took them and opened the door.

"Bracie, I'm sorry this happened. Look at me Bracie."

When she lifted her head, tears fell down her cheeks. Tyler reached down and kissed her. She stood there, scared to enjoy his touch. Tyler could not bear seeing the look of shame on her face; he hugged her tightly and told her, "I'm sorry Bracie."

He turned and closed the door behind him. Bracie sat in her chair and cried until she couldn't cry any more.

"Oh God, I am so sorry," she kept saying. Bracie finally got up and went into her room. She crawled into bed with her clothes on and went to sleep.

Chapter Thirteen

The next few weeks Bracie stayed in seclusion as much as possible. Her family noticed right away something was wrong. Anthany was furious! D'john and her brothers tried to keep him as calm as possible. They were not doing a good job.

"Carl wanted to get her in bed; when she said no, he dumped her. That's what happened, and I know it is!" he yelled.

"Dang man, if they love each other, it would have been okay, it wasn't gonna hurt nobody," Raymond said.

Everyone looked at him and said, "Shut up!"

"Hey, I'm just saying, she's 52 years old and being with someone she loves is not the end of the world. It would be better than the crap she is feeling right now!"

D'john looked at her brother, "I understand what you are saying, but you know Mama, she is who she is."

"I knew this was going to happen," Anthany said frustrated. "I know Mama told him up front, and he thought all those gifts would make her give in. I tried to tell her, but she wouldn't listen!"

Romesha touched her husband on the shoulder to try and comfort him. "We all love Mama, but she makes her own decisions. She'll be okay, she will bounce back. When have you known her not to?" Everyone knew Anthany was angry because he felt like he had not protected her.

Everyone at T. Wahs Production was on edge. After Tyler's weekend in Austin, he came back mean and distracted. He was giving out wrong cues and getting angry over nothing in particular most of the time. After a few weeks of not progressing on the movie, he told everyone to take the weekend off. Tyler walked out of the studio and went home.

He stopped in the kitchen to look at pictures that had been put there by Cora. They were pictures of him and Bracie on Christmas. He was still standing there when Shanelle came in.

"Tyler, call her. You are distracted and frustrated, and you are taking it out on everyone around you."

Tyler looked at her, but did not say anything.

"I don't know what happened, but I do know you are in love with her. Look what being away from her is doing to you. Bracie is in your heart; she loves you Tyler, call her." Shanelle walked over to Tyler and hugged him. "You need her, brother, call her."

Tyler knew she was right, but could not pick up the phone.

Bracie

At the studio, Tyler's pain was evident to everyone but Greg. He didn't know what happened, and he didn't care. He was glad Bracie was out of the picture. Tyler had become consumed with her and that was not good in his book. He'll get over her and move on. He always does. Greg's pride rose up because he didn't have to intervene this time.

Bracie's family was meeting at Dave and Buster's to hangout. She always had fun there, so she got dressed to go. They needed to see that she was all right. Bracie reached over and turned on the television while she finished dressing. There was Tyler with a woman on his arm. This time, Bracie felt the sting. Fresh tears rolled down her face.

Her family was watching the television when Necia walked up to Romesha,

"Mama, that is Mr. Tyler. He was at grandma's house."

Some of them laughed, but none made jokes in fear of Anthany's attitude.

"I told y'all about the jokes; now you have my daughter believing that bull," Romesha told them. "And no jokes when mama gets here."

Necia went over to her great-grandmother.

"Mama, Mr. Tyler was at grandma's for real," she said.

Ms. Deanie hugged Necia and told her, "I know baby, I believe you, now go and play." Necia smiled and went to play with her cousins.

Bracie picked up her phone and dialed.

"Shanelle, I just saw Tyler on television. Did you know about the woman that was on his arm? I thought you were my friend. I feel like a fool. You all know I love Tyler, and you knew he was seeing someone else," Bracie said with tears in her eyes.

"Bracie please don't cry. It's not what it seems. She walked up right before the camera went on." Shanelle tried to explain.

"Yeah, I believe that, bye," Bracie said and hung up the phone.

Carl looked at Shanelle, Bracie seems to be taking this just as hard as Tyler. Shanelle nodded as tears filled her eyes. Carl held her in his arms and comforted her. Shanelle had become very fond of Bracie and hated that she thought ill of her. Bracie sat down and cried. Soon she got herself together and went to be with her family. I'm going to have a good time tonight if it kills me, she thought and walked through the door.

Valentines' Day had come and gone and Bracie felt lost and empty. John told her this would happen if she wasn't careful. She kept hearing his words "Stop beating yourself up, you are human and you have human needs. Pain does not have an age limit," he'd told her. Bracie shook her head as she thought about his last visit. He held her and listened as she told him what happened. How many times had he held her when her heart was

Bracie

broken? It was never like this. She cried so, until it seemed like he was crying with her. John put her to bed and sat there until she finally went to sleep. He kissed her on top of the head and let himself out.

"Man!" he said as he locked the door and pulled out his phone.

Tyler had been at the studio for hours getting things ready for the Austin shoot. He sat there not knowing what to do about Bracie. He understood he loved her, but he needed to give her time, how much time he did not know. He turned back to the screen and deposited $5,000 into Bracie's account. He still felt the need to make sure she was taken care of, he had been depositing money into her account every month since December. When he looked up from the screen Carl was standing there.

"I didn't hear you come in." Tyler said to him.

Carl looked at Tyler, "I know we are like brothers and I don't usually tell you what to do."

"Spit it out Carl," Tyler told him in frustration.

"You need to get things right with Ms. Bracie." He told Tyler about the phone call and how much it hurt Shanelle. Tyler apologized and told Carl he would talk to Shanelle soon. Tyler thought about Carl coming to Shanelle's aid when she needed someone and laughed at the thought of them as a couple.

Tyler went back to work when someone knocked on his door. Assuming it was Carl again he shouted, "Come on in, man!"

"May I help you?" Tyler asked.

The man stuck his hand out and said, "My name is John Wright, and I am a close friend of Bracie's."

Tyler shook his hand and told him to have a seat; he was afraid something was wrong with Bracie. Then he remembered the phone call Christmas morning. So this is John, he thought.

Bracie sat at home enjoying some of her favorite jazz by candlelight. Romesha knocked on her door. Bracie wasn't expecting anyone so she moved slowly to open the door.

"Hello, daughter what's up?"

"I came to check on you," she said. They laughed and said, "Anthany" at the same time. Bracie went and sat in her chair with one foot under her.

"Mama what happened?"

"I'll talk about it later," she said.

"Well, can I see this doll you and your granddaughter keep talking about?" Bracie went into her room and brought the doll to Romesha.

"Wow, she is beautiful!" Romesha examined all the detailed work that went into the doll and her ensemble. "Someone paid a lot of money for this doll. You can tell she was specially made."

Bracie laughed, because she never gave that much thought.

Bracie

"Now, may I ask, why did you want a doll at 52 years old?"

Bracie smiled as she took the doll from Romesha and held her like a baby.

"When I was younger, I had a doll that I loved. It was so beautiful, but nothing compared to this. Anyway during one of our moves, the doll got lost. Since I already had D'john, no one seemed to realize how much the doll meant to me. I asked for a black doll every Christmas for about 15 years and no one took me seriously. By the time I met Matthew, I had stopped mentioning it. I guess the inner child still wanted her doll."

"I guess," Romesha said and they both laughed.

Bracie asked Romesha to put the doll back on her bed. Romesha put the doll down and picked up the picture frame off of her nightstand.

Bracie looked up as Romesha walked out of her room with Tyler's picture.

"This is Tyler Shaw, and this picture was taken here in your chair!"

Bracie chuckled at the look on her face.

"I owe my baby an apology; she was telling the truth," Romesha said.

"So your breakup was with Tyler and not Carl?" Bracie nodded yes.

"Then who is Carl?" Bracie smiled and told her, Tyler's driver.

"Wow, how long has this been going on?"

The expression on Romesha's face made Bracie really laugh when she told her over seven months. Romesha was still teasing Bracie when someone knocked on the door.

"Oh that is probably D'john; she's suppose to meet me here," Romesha said as Bracie got up. She opened the door, and Tyler was standing there with a dozen yellow roses.

"Come in," Bracie said.

"A peace offering," Tyler said as he gave her the roses.

"OMG!" Romesha made both of them turn. Bracie introduced them to each other. Romesha gave Tyler a small grin.

"Do you need me to stay, mama?" she asked.

They laughed, but Tyler and Bracie knew she was serious.

"No, I'll be fine," Bracie replied.

Tyler looked at Romesha and asked her for a favor.

"I don't know you like that, for you to be asking for favors and stuff," she answered.

Bracie laughed and told her to listen because she wanted to hear what the favor was, too.

"Can you get your family over to your home tomorrow evening? I think it's about time for everyone to know I'm in love with Bracie. We can't move forward as long as we keep this a secret."

Bracie sat down in shock.

Tyler turned to her and asked, "Is that okay with you?"

Bracie

Bracie only nodded. Tyler saw Romesha out and locked the door.

Tyler pulled Bracie out of the chair and hugged her tight. "My baby. I am so sorry. Please forgive me for breaking my promise," Tyler told her.

"I was at fault, too," she said.

Tyler sat her back in the chair and kneeled in front of her.

"Bracie, the one thing I learned in these past few weeks is, I absolutely cannot live without you."

He took her hand and asked her, "Will you marry me, Bracie? Will you do me the honor of being Mrs. Tyler Shaw?"

"Yes," Bracie cried with tears streaming down her face. This time, they were tears of joy.

Tyler took the ring out of his pocket and slid it on her left hand. He took her by the hand and they sat on the sofa. Bracie moved away. Tyler understood, but he was still hurt by her actions.

"Bracie, when I said I was sorry I was talking about what happened in Austin, not for our relationship."

She looked at Tyler and told him, "I thought you were saying you couldn't stay in the relationship if we could not sleep together."

"Oh, my angel, I wanted to give you time to get over what happened. The look on your face was devastating, and I didn't want to rush my feelings upon you. I am very much in love with you Bracie Turner, and I never want to live without you again."

Beulah Neveu

They hugged each other and silently prayed for what God was giving them, a second chance at their relationship. They talked for a while and Tyler stood so he could leave.

"I have a room close by," he told her. He knew staying at her place would not be a good idea. "I will be here around five so we can go to your son's."

Bracie walked Tyler to the door and kissed him goodnight.

Chapter Fourteen

Bracie and Tyler slept peacefully. They both needed the rest that took over as soon as their heads hit their pillows.

Tyler called Bracie early the next morning.

"Hey baby," she answered.

Tyler laughed, because those words were priceless coming from her. They talked for awhile and Tyler told her he would see her later. Bracie looked at her ring and smiled, she would be Mrs. Tyler Shaw. *"Oh God, help me through this. As much as I love Tyler, I cannot do this alone. Bless me to be the wife that you would have me to be. Bless me to love Tyler like you love Tyler and no matter what circumstances may arise, guide me through them as you see fit. May all that I do and say bring honor and glory to you. Thank you Father, Amen."*

When Tyler arrived at Bracie's, she was excited and nervous. Anthany would soon know it was Tyler who hurt her.

He would not be as accepting of Tyler's apology as everyone else. Bracie knew her son well and prayed for God to soften his heart. Tyler and Bracie talked for awhile; they looked at the clock and decided it was time to go. The ride there was quiet. Neither one knew what to expect. When they pulled up, Bracie glanced at each family member's car so she could figure out who was inside. Tyler took Bracie's hand and slid her ring off. She looked at him confused.

"What?" Tyler touched Bracie's lips with his finger, "It's okay; I don't want to give Anthany another reason to be angry with me. As the eldest son, let us talk first. It's a man thing, Bracie; it's respect for his position in your life."

Bracie nodded, "I understand," she said. "Now let's get this over so I can put my ring back where it belongs."

They laughed as they got out of the car. Romesha met them at the front door. Everyone was quiet when Bracie walked in with Tyler.

"Hi Mr. Tyler," Necia said as she ran over and gave him a hug.

"Hello Necia you've gotten taller since I've seen you," Tyler said as he bent down to hug her.

"WTH!" Raymond and Andre' said at the same time.

"Thank you, Romesha," Tyler said and everyone turned and looked at her.

"You knew!" they all said.

"Hey I just found out last night," she replied.

Bracie

Bracie's first two introductions were to her mom and then to Anthany. After she formally introduced him to everyone, they all had questions. The first of course was, who is Carl?

"My driver," Tyler answered.

Anthany looked over at his mom because she purposely let everyone believe Carl was her boyfriend. Trevion and LeAndre couldn't believe their grandmother had been dating Tyler Shaw, the famous movie producer/director all this time.

"I can't wait until school Monday," they both said.

John had warned Tyler about Anthany and how protective he was of his mother. The fact that she had been hurt made him watch her even closer. "If you can get through to him you got it made," John told him. Tyler figured it's now or never and asked if he could speak to Anthany alone. Bracie, Romesha, and D'john stopped what they were doing and looked up. They all saw the look of concern on Bracie's face as the two men walked outside. Ms. Deanie walked over to her daughter.

"It's going to be fine, Bracie. I had a talk with Anthany this morning after Romesha called. He already knew it was Tyler."

Bracie hugged her mom and told her thank you.

"That's what moms are for, paving the way," she said as Francine and Randy walked up. They all listened as Bracie told them about how they met and about the trips they had taken together. She skipped the details of their Austin trip, but told them it was a miscommunication on both of their parts. Bracie was happy, so her family was happy.

Beulah Neveu

No one realized it had been over an hour since Anthany and Tyler left the room. Bracie was relieved when they entered with no battle armor drawn. Anthany asked for everyone's attention. When they all stopped and turned his way he gave the floor to Tyler. Tyler reached into his pocket and took out Bracie's ring. In front of her family he proposed for the second time and for the second time she said yes. Bracie walked over and hugged her mother.

"Be happy, Bracie," she told her daughter.

Ms. Deanie had mixed emotions right then. She and Bracie were very close, and she knew Bracie marrying Tyler would take her daughter miles from home. The ladies surrounded Bracie and the men grilled Tyler. When they finally said goodnight, Bracie was exhausted.

Tyler closed the door behind them and locked it. Bracie sat next to him on the sofa and put her head on his shoulder.

"Tyler, you know this will be all over Houston in about two hours."

He laughed, "Yeah, I know. I hope you can handle it. I'm used to the media."

Bracie laughed now. "I guess you are right," she said. She looked at her ring again and said thank you.

"For?" he asked.

"A beautiful ring with such a dainty diamond. It's me. It's not too big; it's just right."

Bracie

Tyler looked down at Bracie and smiled. "You are welcome," he said. Tyler knew she meant that from her heart because he could tell she had no idea how much her ring cost. Wait until she sees the band he thought. The set cost him close to 20 grand.

"So I can leave it on now?" she asked.

"Of course. Everyone that matters knows. The media is the media; they will make of it whatever they want. You be careful of your local media, because they will find you as soon as they realize we really are engaged." Bracie took a deep breath and moved closer to Tyler. "I'm ready," she said.

"Okay," he replied.

Tyler and Bracie sat quietly for a moment and dozed off. When he woke up, Bracie was sleeping soundly with her head on his lap. Tyler caressed the side of her face and watched her sleep. "How can someone who is this beautiful, be 52 years old and still innocent in her own way?" he asked himself. She loves from her heart, not with her eyes, he thought and bent down to kiss the side of her face. Tyler woke Bracie up and told her to lock the door. She kissed him goodnight, showered, and went to bed.

Bracie got up early and made a pot of coffee. She sat at the table and thought about the last nine months of her life. She finished her coffee and went into her bedroom to get dressed for church. When she arrived she went into the choir room to have prayer with the praise team. After prayer they went to their place on the stage and waited for the musicians.

"That's Tyler Shaw," she heard one of the members say.

Bracie looked up and there he was, waiting for service to begin. He had remembered where Bracie told him she usually sat on Sunday morning. The music started and Bracie had to put her focus on the Father. "Remember to Whom you are singing," Oliver told them each Sunday before they stepped in front of the congregation. Praise and Worship was spirit filled as usual. After they left the stage, Bracie went and sat next to Tyler.

"Why didn't you tell me you were coming?" She asked.

"Surprise," he said with a smile.

Bracie knew at this moment all eyes were on her. Ms. Deanie looked at the two of them smiling. She knew Bracie was happy and excited because she could finally be open about her relationship with Tyler. Necia came and sat next to Tyler and gave him a hug. Sheila brought Shani to Bracie and gave her the 'you are so in trouble' look. They smiled as Shani lay in her godmother's arms. Tyler put his arm around Bracie, and they enjoyed the service. The baby was still asleep when Charles and Sheila came over to Bracie and Tyler.

"Well, what is this?" she asked as soon as Bracie formally introduced them.

"This is me and Tyler," she said laughing.

"See, having a baby has me so out of touch," Sheila laughed.

"We have to hangout soon," Bracie told her.

Bracie

Sheila agreed as she and Charles left. Tyler and Bracie went to speak to her pastors. She introduced them to Tyler, but he had met them both before at a fundraising event. They were surprised to see him with Bracie, but they were glad to see her so happy. Bracie put her hand out for the first time so they could see her ring. Both of her pastors congratulated them on their engagement. Pastor Brooks asked them to step into his office so he could pray for them.

Bracie gave her keys to Raymond and told him to drive her car to his grandmother's. Tyler and Bracie got in his car to leave when she saw John's truck.

"Pull into that driveway," she said.

"Who lives here?" he asked.

"My best friend," Bracie replied.

"I thought that was Sheila."

"Easy misconception," she smiled as she pulled out her phone. John walked out as he hung up the phone. Tyler got out and opened Bracie's door.

She introduced them, "John this is Tyler, Tyler this is my best friend, John."

As the men reached to shake hands Bracie's phone went off.

"Excuse me," she said and took a few steps over.

"Thank you," Tyler told John. "I had no idea she thought I walked out on her."

John looked at Tyler, "Take care of her, she loves you."

Tyler nodded, "I promise. I asked her to marry me, and she said yes."

Bracie walked up, "And what are you two talking about?"

"Just man talk," they said.

Bracie stuck her left hand out so John could see her ring. "Congratulations," he told her and gave Bracie his John bear hug. Tyler and a few of her church members watched as John hugged Bracie and kiss her on top of the head. Tyler could see now why John had gotten on a plane to come see him. Bracie not only trusted him, she loved him.

Chapter Fifteen

The news of Tyler's engagement spread through the Production Studio very fast. Everyone was excited and work on the movie progressed well. At the end of the day, Tyler told everyone that for the next two weeks they would be filming in Austin, Texas.

"Come focused and ready to work; they only gave us ten working days so we have to get this done. We had a great week, have an even greater weekend, and I'll see you all Monday in the big state of Texas."

Shanelle was very happy to see Tyler excited about his engagement. Greg came out of his office and sunk her spirits.

"Congratulations, Tyler," Greg said while shaking his hand.

"Thank you," Tyler answered back.

Shanelle knew Greg would be up to no good, she just didn't know how. Tyler left the studio and went straight to the airport.

Later that night, Tyler was standing on Bracie's porch knocking on the door. Bracie let Tyler in and kissed him. They ate a light dinner and went into the living room.

"Bracie, how long do you want to wait before we get married?"

She didn't know what to say because she was not expecting the question.

"Ah, six months?" she was asking more than stating.

"Six months!" Tyler said rather abruptly.

Misunderstanding his tone Bracie said, "Ok, a year?"

Shaking his head Tyler said, "A year? No baby we can't do any one of those!"

Bracie looked at Tyler confused. "What do you want?" she asked softly.

Tyler realized he had given her the wrong impression by his response and settled down. He held Bracie's face in his hand and kissed her softly on the lips.

"You have six weeks Bracie Turner to put a wedding together."

She almost choked, "Six weeks?"

Tyler looked her in the eyes and told her, "In six weeks you will be my wife, because in six weeks I am going to make love to you. A wedding or standing before a judge, it is up to you, but you have only six weeks to get it done and not one day more, you understand me Bracie?"

She nodded her head yes.

Bracie

"I'm staying here for the weekend, and I will be leaving for Austin Sunday evening. Is that okay with you?"

Again Bracie nodded her head yes. Bracie gave Tyler his pajamas and a set of towels as he headed for the shower.

While Tyler was in the bathroom, Bracie cleaned the kitchen. When she opened the closet to get out the inflatable bed, Tyler told her not to. Bracie stood up and lowered her head.

"I love you Bracie, what happened in Austin will not happen again." Tyler lifted her chin so she could look at him. "It happened, it's over, and we have to let it go, ok?"

Bracie nodded yes. "Do you trust me, Bracie?"

"Yes," she whispered. "I will never hurt you or do anything to take away your trust. I promise that to you Bracie." He held her in his arms. "It's late, let's go to bed."

Tyler closed the closet door and they went into Bracie's bedroom. She put her doll on the chaise while Tyler turned the covers down. Bracie stood at the foot of the bed and folded her arms. Tyler came behind Bracie and put his arms around her.

"It's fine baby, I understand the last man that slept in this bed was Matthew."

Bracie turned and looked at him.

"He's not angry Bracie, because he knows I love you; he knows you are going to be taken care of."

Bracie hugged Tyler and walked to her side of the bed. She turned out the lights, got into bed, and lay in Tyler's arms. Bracie felt safe, she felt secure, and she felt loved.

Tyler was up early. The last time he slept that well was Christmas Eve. He let Bracie sleep as he went over some of his paper work. Something didn't look right on his financial spreadsheet, but he could not pinpoint it. I'll look into it later, he thought and wrote a note at the top of the page. He put everything back into his brief case and started breakfast.

The smell of coffee woke Bracie up. She went into the restroom to freshen up. Bracie walked into the kitchen and kissed Tyler good morning. She helped finish breakfast and they sat down to eat.

Bracie and Tyler decided to stay in for the day. They laughed and talked a lot. They looked through most of her photo albums and scrap books. Bracie went into the bedroom and brought out three beautiful books you could tell she spent a lot of time and effort on. They were from their weekends together and Christmas. They flipped each page carefully and commented on every picture. Tyler realized just how many pictures she had of them together and none of them ever made it to the press. She had kept her promise, too.

Bracie

Tyler lay in bed that night listening to Bracie breathe as she slept. Tyler did something he had not done in a long time, he prayed.

"Father, it's me, Tyler. I know it has been a while, but I see you have not forgotten me. Will you show me how to love Bracie? Her heart is tender, Lord, and she is so beautiful inside and out. Help me to do what is right for her. I am new at this love thing, but I do know what I feel for her is true, and it is real. I cannot do this by myself; I need you Father. Amen." He hugged Bracie and went to sleep.

Tyler and Bracie went to church and then to Ms. Deanie's for dinner. They were sitting at the table when Je'Keith walked up. He smiled at his grandmother and they went through their usual routine. Bracie held his fingers to her lips as Tyler watched her. Bracie had all of her attention focused on her grandson.

"You can do it, say grandma."

Je'Keith made sounds and smiled at Bracie when she gave him a hug. He stepped over in front of Tyler, looked at him, smiled, and walked off. Tyler kept his eyes on Je'Keith for the rest of the visit. Every now and then Je'Keith would look at Tyler and smile.

"Ms. Deanie, do you cook like this every Sunday?"

"Yes, I do," she said, "but from this day on you are to call me Mama Deanie or just Mama will do. You are a member of the family now."

Tyler smiled at her and said thank you.

"Have you two set a date yet?" Romesha asked.

"Yeah, Tyler wants us to get married in six weeks."

"SIX WEEKS?"

Bracie laughed, "Exactly!"

"We need to get busy," D'john said. "I guess the first question should be, where will you get married?"

Bracie turned and looked at Tyler.

"Houston is fine as long as you get it done in that time frame."

"Colors?" asked Romesha.

He looked at Bracie, "This is your baby, and you can have whatever colors you want."

"Well, what is her spending limit?" D'john asked sarcastically.

Tyler looked at all three ladies, "There is no limit; whatever Bracie wants, as long as it is done in six weeks."

He got up and walked outside to talk with the other men. Raymond was standing there and became curious as to why Tyler was so persistent about marrying his mom in six weeks. Tyler and Bracie stayed a little while longer and left. Tyler took Bracie home, kissed her, and headed to Austin.

D'john, Romesha, and Sheila were waiting for Bracie at Ms. Deanie's to start on her wedding plans. I wonder why he wants this to happen so fast, the ladies questioned among themselves. Ms. Deanie answered all their questions at one time.

Bracie

"He is ready to make love to her, and that's the only way it's going to happen."

"Grandma," they all laughed.

"What's so funny?" Bracie asked as she walked into the dining room.

"Your mama is tripping."

"About what?" Bracie asked.

They didn't know if they should repeat what they had been saying. Bracie put her hands in the air, "About what?"

Romesha spoke up, "We were wondering why Tyler wanted to get married so quick."

Bracie laughed, "Oh that is easy, he's horny."

They all laughed and got down to business.

"Six weeks from now is May 7th.:

They sat around the calendar looking at dates. Bracie got out her datebook and realized she had promised Vanessa she would speak to her young ladies group on that day. Tyler couldn't be reached so Bracie set the date for Saturday, May 14th.

"Ok, let's move on to colors."

They looked at twenty different colors before Bracie decided on turquoise and ivory.

"We need to find a venue that can host the wedding and reception. We need a guest list; we need a caterer, a photographer, video, and…"

Bracie sat quietly while it seemed like that list of things would not stop. The ladies gathered around her.

You have us, and we are going to get this done," D'john said.

She was right. They had to make sure everyone would be available for that day and time. Bracie told the ladies she had to stop at the daycare and turn in her resignation. It was hard to do it without notice, but it had to be done to pull this off in six weeks and prepare to speak to the group of young ladies.

The group got into Romesha's Expedition and went to find a place for Bracie's wedding. After they booked a hotel in the Galleria, they rode to South Park to eat at Hick's. Terry greeted them at the door with a smile and a load of pictures. His wife had given birth to a beautiful baby girl on Valentine's Day. The ladies finished eating and got back to work; six weeks was not a lot of time.

Bracie sat up waiting for Tyler. He finished filming a day early so they would spend the weekend together. His knock brought a smile to her face. Tyler kissed Bracie and told her they could go over details of the wedding after he showered. Bracie put everything on the living room table so they could cuddle near the sofa. Bracie fixed Tyler a light dinner and had it waiting when he came into the living room. He sat on the floor with Bracie and ate while she talked.

"Hey, hey back up, May 14th is passed six weeks."

Bracie

Bracie was hoping he didn't catch that, but she should have known better. She explained about the speaking engagement that she didn't want to decline. Tyler agreed on the date because he forgot he had to attend an awards dinner the week before. He looked around and asked Bracie when she wanted to start moving her things.

"As soon as possible," she answered.

Tyler touched Bracie's hand, "I booked you a flight out with me Sunday evening so we can make some changes around the house to fit your things in." He kissed her and picked up the material on the table.

"Nice color. I like it," he said. They decided on three bridal attendants and three groomsmen each. Tyler chose his three right away - Carl, John, and Greg.

"John? My friend John?" Bracie asked.

"Our friend John," Tyler replied. He knew that would make her happy. "Now what three ladies are you going to choose?" he asked.

"I don't know, it's so hard," Bracie said concerned about the short notice she would have to give.

Tyler shook his head and said, "D'john, Sheila, and Shanelle. See how simple that was?" They both laughed and Bracie agreed with his choice. Tyler put his plate in the sink, and he and Bracie went to bed.

Carl met Tyler and Bracie at the airport. Shanelle was waiting for them at the house. By the time Tyler put Bracie's bags on her bed, she and Shanelle were buried in wedding books. After a while Bracie pushed all the books aside.

"They are all beautiful, but none of them are me."

Shanelle sat next to Bracie, "Girlfriend, you are marrying one of the wealthiest men in America. People will expect for you to wear a designer gown."

"I hate to disappoint," said Bracie, "but I don't want to wear a designer gown. I want something that says me, beautiful yet simple."

Shanelle shook her head at Bracie while smiling the whole time.

Tyler came into the sitting room to get Bracie. They stood in the middle of the room while Tyler pointed out three doors to her. Bracie always wondered what was behind the doors that were in the main sitting room.

Tyler pointed to the first door. "That is my office, my space. The second door is somewhat of a storage room, and this Bracie, is your space." He opened the door to a very large room.

Shanelle walked over with a pen and pad and told Bracie, "Now let us get to work on your space." Bracie asked Tyler if one complete wall could be bookshelves.

"I teach and speak a lot, so I have a large assortment of books, Bibles, and study material," she told him.

Bracie

"It's your space, do with it as you like. Now I'm going to leave you in the capable hands of Shanelle." Tyler and Carl left the ladies alone and headed out the door.

Shanelle and Bracie spent all day Monday and Tuesday designing her room and ordering furniture. Tyler helped her choose a beautiful cherry wood desk. When Bracie saw the price, she tried to get a different desk, but Tyler wouldn't hear of it. Bracie stood in the middle of the room and imagined where her chair and chaise would go.

Tyler left early for the studio. Bracie was heading into the kitchen when she heard voices. When she saw Shanelle and Carl, she stopped. She knew right away it was an intimate meeting. Carl caressed Shanelle's face and kissed her. Bracie smiled, turned, and went back upstairs to get dressed.

Shanelle and Vanessa were helping Bracie find something special to wear for her wedding.

"Girlfriend, you are difficult," Vanessa said. "Most women would have chosen a $50,000 gown by now, just because they are marrying Tyler Shaw, and you got us out here trying to find something that is you," she said.

"I know and I'm sorry. I'm marrying the man of my dreams so I need the dress of my dreams, and I don't think it is coming out of a designer's book," Bracie told them.

Vanessa and Shanelle both agreed. "You are going to drive Tyler crazy. You are so down to earth, it's unbelievable.

Bracie laughed and said, "He knows, believe me he knows; now let's go to Jana's," and off they went.

Jana hugged Bracie and congratulated her on her engagement. "I need to see your three most beautiful off white suits or dresses," Bracie said, "Oh and Jana, this time the price tag does not matter."

Jana smiled and went to find a few ensembles for Bracie to choose from. Bracie looked at several of the outfits, when she saw the suit she wanted to wear. The Brocade jacket had pearls around the bottom hem and collar. The matching silk floor length skirt had a split up the front with crushed pearl accents around the split and hem.

"It's you Bracie," they all said.

"What is this for?" Jana asked.

"It's my wedding suit," Bracie said with a smile.

"I am honored," Jana replied. She had Bracie try the suit on so she could take her measurements. "When you find your shoes, bring them in so I can mark your hem," Jana told Bracie.

"Well that's done, let's keep moving," and they were out of the door."

Bracie

Bracie sat outside thinking about the move to California. She would be away from her family for the first time in her life. Bracie waited until she was fifty-two to make one of the biggest changes of her life, and she was more than a little nervous. Tyler found her sitting in the garden and sat with her.

"Nervous?" he asked.

"Somewhat," she confessed.

"It shows," Tyler told her.

Dang, I got to work on that, Bracie thought to herself.

"You up for dinner and dancing tonight?"

"Why sure!" Bracie replied.

"Gail and Larry invited us to their yacht this evening." Tyler laughed when Bracie's face lit up like a little kid. "Casual and comfortable is the attire."

Tyler and Bracie spent the rest of their afternoon in the garden.

"Nice pool," Bracie commented.

"Thanks, I can't wait until it warms up so we can take a swim," he said.

"Yeah right, a swim," Bracie said laughing. Tyler cut his eyes at her and laughed too.

Tyler and Bracie arrived at the Yacht Club the same time as Vanessa and Josh. They all spoke and went to the yacht together. Greg and Angela were already onboard with a few other guests. Gail and Larry were wonderful hosts; they informed everyone the yacht would pull out into deeper water right before dinner. They had a live five-piece band playing on deck so everyone gathered there after dinner. Tyler and Bracie stood at the railing of the yacht looking at the beautiful scenery.

"I love you, Tyler," Bracie said.

He turned Bracie towards him, "I love you too, Bracie." He took her into his arms and kissed her. Everyone was sitting around laughing and talking, glad to see Tyler happy.

Vanessa looked at Greg and shook her head. "Why you have to be so jealous?" she asked Greg.

"Mind your own business!" he replied. Before Vanessa could say anything else, Josh told her not to start, not tonight! Vanessa made it a known fact, that Greg was not one of her favorite people. She and Greg glared at each other and Vanessa walked off. The ladies went inside and left the men out on deck.

"Why is Shanelle not here?" Bracie asked.

Gail told them Shanelle declined the invitation when she heard Greg would be there.

"Sorry, Angela," she said.

Angela knew Greg was no good; she said so herself on many occasions. She was only buying her time with him now. Angela knew too much about Greg to ever be happy with him.

The ladies went outside while Bracie went into the restroom. When she came out Greg was waiting to go in. Bracie looked at the small space and told Greg to come on through, but he told

Bracie

her to come out first. As Bracie moved through Greg moved in behind her and leaned in against her. That pissed Bracie off!

Tyler asked if anything was wrong the moment she stepped on the deck.

"No," she lied.

Greg smiled at her when he came back, too soon to say he actually used it. Bracie turned her head from him and stayed next to Tyler.

Chapter Sixteen

Bracie flew back to Houston alone. Sheila picked her up from the airport.

"I'm ready; I have no luggage."

"What happened to it?" Sheila asked.

"I left it at Tyler's. That's less I will have to pack up," Bracie said while playing with her godbaby and snapping pictures of her.

Once Sheila dropped Bracie at home, Bracie decided to stay in for the rest of the day. She was still angry with Greg for the stunt he pulled on the yacht. "He's up to no good; I can feel it."

Greg took Bracie's silence the wrong way. "She's just like the other whores Tyler dated," he thought. "They would do anything to get the things they wanted, even sleep with me. Bracie liked what I did. Now that I know she is like the rest of them, I will reel her in slowly, but she, I will humiliate," he

Bracie

thought with a smile. Greg was so full of himself he really did not notice the glare Bracie had in her eyes.

The weeks seemed to fly by. Ms. Deanie and all the ladies of Bracie's family came to help her pack. Deciding what to take with her made for some rough moments. Bracie put her wedding album with Matthew into a box. She picked up the only picture of them she still had out, placed it carefully into the box also, and taped the edges. She put it with the stuff to take to California. They all looked, but D'john asked her if she was sure she wanted to take those with her.

"Yes, these are memories I don't trust to be anywhere else, but with me." Bracie looked at the box, took a deep breath, and went back to sorting through her things. Bracie only packed two pieces of furniture, her favorite chair and the chaise from her bedroom, both were gifts from Matthew that she would not part with. Her bedroom she put in an empty room at her mother's and everyone else chose what they wanted or needed. Once everything was loaded and the apartment locked up, Bracie breathed a sigh of relief. Tyler had taken care of all the flight arrangements and the cargo should arrive at his home later in the week. Trevion pulled up to his grandmother's apartment and saw she had everything packed.

"Grandma, will you be back for my graduation?" he asked.

Bracie hugged him, "You are my oldest grandchild and nothing will keep me away on your big day. I already have June

4th marked on my calendar." This will be a big event for their family. Trevion is Ms. Deanie's first great grandchild, so he will be the first graduate of his generation.

D'john, Romesha, and Shanelle, sat at the table with Bracie to finalize all of the details of the wedding. Shanelle fit right in with the family, and she loved it. She watched and was amazed at how close they were to be such a large family. Shanelle flew in with Bracie's suit that Friday and spent the weekend in Houston. Everyone loved Bracie's suit. They got together and found the perfect shoes. Shanelle's last responsibility was security, and that had to be perfect for she and Bracie would be flying out Tuesday morning.

Romesha and Shanelle stayed in touch about the wedding plans so Bracie would not have to worry. Bracie was exhausted. Tyler hired professional movers to unpack her cargo crate, but arranging everything was still tiring. Bracie's clothes had been carefully put on Tyler's bed and all of her shoes and purses were stacked to one side. She was standing at the door when Tyler walked up behind her. "It's okay to go in," he teased.

"I have not been in your bedroom before," she said.

He wrapped his arms around her and whispered in her ear. "Our bedroom, my love, our bedroom. Now come on and let's put your things away." For the next three hours Tyler and Bracie arranged her sections of the closet.

Chapter Seventeen

May 6th seemed to have arrived too soon. Bracie sat on her bed looking at her blue dress. She flew home last Saturday evening for the final fitting for both dresses. Francine fixed her hair and showed her how to style it for tonight.

"You nervous?" she asked her sister.

"Very," Bracie said. "I guess the world will see Bracie Turner for the first time Friday night." Francine tried to assure her everything would be alright. Now Bracie sat there trying not to be nervous, but she wasn't doing a good job of it. She looked at the clock and got up to get dressed.

Tyler, Shanelle, and Carl were waiting for her at the bottom of the staircase. All three were speechless as she walked down the stairs. Bracie took Tyler's arm and they all left. When they arrived at the hotel, Tyler could tell Bracie was nervous. He kissed her hand and told her, "It's ok, hold on to me."

Everyone in Bracie's family sat in front of the television at Ms. Deanie's to watch her first big public appearance. John was on the road, but he pulled over to watch also.

"Give it to them, Bracie," he said out loud, but to himself. Dwayne sat in front of his television. "My Bracie," he thought then realized he had claimed a part of her. They announced Tyler's limo as Carl got out to open the door. Tyler stepped out first and Bracie could see the media all around him. Tyler reached in and took Shanelle's hand first. Bracie turned and when her feet were stable, she took Tyler's hand and stood up out of the limo. The lights from the cameras were blinding. She stood there, Tyler stepped closer to her and touched her at the base of her back.

"Let's go, baby," he said as he held on to Bracie as she took her first walk under the big lights.

When Bracie stood up, the house went completely silent for a moment.

"Wow, look at grandma, she is beautiful!" Trevion said very excited.

The announcer said, "It seems Tyler Shaw went to Houston and found himself an angel. I wonder what designer is taking credit for this stunning gown she has on? It goes with the sapphire and diamond pendant and bracelet she is wearing."

They seemed to notice everything she had on. When one announcer stopped Tyler to ask about the woman on his arm,

Bracie seemed to glow when he answered, "This is my fiancée, Bracie Turner."

He turned and they walked inside.

Every phone in Ms. Deanie's house started ringing. John just sit there looking. In all his years of knowing Bracie, he had never seen her look so beautiful.

Once inside, Bracie didn't have to worry about cameras anymore. The dinner was good and so was the company, but she was glad to be back in the limo on her way home. Home, this is home now, she thought.

Once inside, Tyler walked Bracie to her room and kissed her goodnight. Bracie went in and undressed. She showered and then realized all of her clothes where in Tyler's room now. She had to get her clothes ready for tomorrow. She knocked on the door.

"Tyler? Tyler?" She heard the shower and realized that's why he didn't answer. Bracie thought she would make a quick dash in the closet, get her things, and get out before Tyler got out of the shower. She thought wrong! She came out of the closet through the wrong door and bumped into Tyler. When Bracie startled him, Tyler dropped his towel. She couldn't move as she looked at him in all of his handsome nakedness.

"Oh My God!" she whispered as her eyes roamed his body. Bracie turned and walked out of the room. Tyler made sure his door was closed before he started laughing.

Bracie sat on her bed breathing hard. She bit her bottom lip so hard, she tasted blood. After a few minutes, Tyler knocked on her door. She got up to open it.

"These belong to you," he handed her the clothes she had gotten out of the closet. "Come get what you need," he took her by the hand and led her back into their bedroom.

Bracie got everything she needed and was headed out the door. Tyler stepped in front of her. Bracie looked up at him. He touched her face.

"Bracie when you leave Monday, you will be coming back to this bedroom. Whenever you like, feel free to come in and get used to being in here."

Bracie nodded and went back to her room. Tyler lay in bed and laughed. "She's 52 and still shy. What a woman and she is all mine," he said as he drifted off to sleep.

Chapter Eighteen

Bracie met Vanessa at the Youth Center. They walked into her room, where thirteen young ladies were waiting for them. At Bracie's request, Vanessa introduced her only as Bracie Turner from Houston, Texas.

"Good morning ladies," Bracie smiled. Some spoke back and others just looked at her.

"Well, let me open by asking a question. Why do you think I am here this morning?" she asked.

"To talk to us," one of the young ladies answered.

"About what?" Bracie put the question back out to them.

They started to respond, "sex or the lack of it," "how not to get into trouble," "respecting ourselves and others," "how to marry a rich man", they all laughed, and "how to be a better person." One young lady just sat there. Bracie noticed she didn't speak nor was she participating now. Bracie asked for her opinion.

She looked up at Bracie with cold eyes. "You came here to judge us and to put us down like everyone else has. Look at you with your fancy suit looking all refined and thinking you got it made with that Tyler Shaw."

"Cherralyn that was disrespectful," Vanessa broke in.

Bracie touched Vanessa and shook her head. "No, I asked her a question, and she gave me an honest answer."

Bracie walked to the middle of the room. "First, I wasn't asked here to judge you, so in like manner, I ask that you not judge me because of my clothes and who I'm engaged to. Cherralyn, I have been called a lot of things in my days, but never refined. I take that as a compliment, so thank you. Now, I heard all of your answers, and I cannot pass judgment on you because God has been forgiving towards me. Most of you said sex or the lack of it. Today we will be transparent. I have been celibate since my first husband passed over three years ago."

All of them looked at Bracie.

Cherralyn spoke up, "So you not hittin' it with Mr. Rich Man?"

"First, his name is Tyler, not Mr. Rich Man, and no ladies, I am not hittin' it or any other terms you all may be using. Before Matthew, I was celibate eight years, but before that I had four children out of wedlock."

"So, you had sex and then you stopped?" one young lady asked very curiously.

"Yes!" Bracie replied.

Bracie

"How did you do that, why did you do that?" they all wanted to know.

Bracie looked at them and told them, "I got tired of thinking some one cared about me just to get me into bed. I had to struggle with my sexuality just like you do. I had to learn sex ain't love and love ain't sex. I had to learn to love me more than any man can. Until you get to the place where you believe you are God's precious daughter, you will continue to give yourself away."

Bracie moved around the room as she continued to talk. "You look at my suit, and you know I am engaged to Tyler Shaw, and you think you know me. Well, I had a life before this suit and Tyler Shaw. I know what it is like to be misused by someone you love. I know what it is to be molested by someone you trust. I have seen the damage abuse causes in the home. Look at me without the suit and see a woman that knows what it means to go to bed hungry so your children can eat. You think it's easy because I love God and I'm a Christian. Well my heart hurts too when someone walks out on me because I stand up for what I believe in."

One young lady raised her hand and Vanessa told her to wait until the end to ask questions. Bracie told Vanessa it was okay.

"Your name?" Bracie asked her.

"Melanie," she replied.

"What is your question, Melanie?"

"Did you love the guy that walked out on you?"

"Back then I thought I did, but it took me awhile to learn it wasn't love. I had to learn that love seeks the greatest good for the one that is loved. Love doesn't purposely hurt, it will allow hurt through discipline, but will be there to strengthen and comfort in the end. Ladies as long as we live we are going to attend the school of life and take courses in Hard Knocks 101."

The young ladies laughed at Bracie's humor, but still paid attention to what she was saying. Cherralyn raised her hand this time and Bracie pointed to her.

"What about the money and the things, you know, gifts."

Bracie walked over and stood in front of Cherralyn, because she could sense there was pain behind her eyes.

"All I can tell you is the truth. I love Tyler, but Tyler Shaw does not have enough money to buy what isn't truly mine to sell. My body is not for sale at any cost. I don't want his money or his things. God provided for me well before I met Tyler. I fell in love with a man not his material possessions. If a guy offers you money or gifts to sleep with him, he does not think much of you at all and even less of himself. You will have to learn to love you for who you are. When you search inside and find the young lady God is calling you to be, you won't accept just anything or anybody."

Bracie pointed to one of the young ladies. "You said be a better person, but be a better person for whom? When you strive to be a better person, you have to do it for you. People change, the only One that I know who does not change is God.

Bracie

Let His Word be your standard. Please know when you become better and begin to do better, everybody is not going to like your change. That's okay, accept it and do even better. God knows how to move people and situations in your life. Sometimes that moving around may hurt, accept the hurt and keep doing better. You have to know and understand, God loves you beyond your mess ups. Whatever you did last night or even this morning, you cannot undo, but you have right now. You can do what you want for your life, starting right now."

The ladies were quiet and focused on Bracie's every word.

"Does anyone have any questions and/or comments?" she asked.

Vanessa stood by in shock at how openly and honestly Bracie answered each question given her.

"Well ladies, my time is almost up, and I have enjoyed this class. Before I leave I want to give you some important advice. Never judge anyone before you get to know them. Always be careful, but never throw stones when you think your house is made of glass. Thank you for having me."

Bracie stepped back and turned the class back over to Vanessa. Cherralyn raised her hand again and Vanessa told her she could make a comment.

"Thank you, Ms. Vanessa for inviting Ms. Turner, and thank you, Ms. Turner for being real with us," she said.

Bracie smiled and acknowledged her comment. Vanessa walked Bracie to the door. "I'll see you tonight at the house," Bracie said to Vanessa as she was leaving.

Bracie was tired, but got through the evening. Vanessa told everyone what a wonderful job Bracie did at the center. Tyler hugged Bracie, "I'm proud of you angel. I hope your talk helped some of those young ladies."

"Me too," she said.

Josh asked Tyler what was different about the room.

Gail told him, "It has Bracie's warmth and touch in here now."

The other guys laughed because they noticed it too but didn't say anything. Bracie kept her eyes on Greg as they all enjoyed the evening; she did not trust him.

Bracie yawned without realizing it.

"All right everyone it's time to go," Vanessa said. "The bride-to-be needs her rest."

Tyler was seeing everyone off while Bracie straightened up the kitchen. Greg walked in.

"Hello Bracie." She looked over at him and didn't say anything.

Shanelle was walking up when Greg walked behind Bracie and tried to kiss her. Bracie turned and slapped Greg so hard he fell back into the refrigerator.

Bracie

"Are you crazy, who the hell do you think you are?" she shouted!

Greg touched the side of his face, "Why you!" he stepped up to Bracie.

"What Greg?" He stepped back when Bracie walked up on him.

"You two bit church tramp," Greg called Bracie.

"If I were one, you wouldn't be standing there just holding your face." Greg walked up on Bracie again, but she still did not back down.

Tyler heard the commotion and headed for the kitchen. Shanelle grabbed him, "Wait," she whispered. Tyler stood to see what was going on with his fiancée and his friend.

"What the hell do you want?" Greg asked!

"I don't want your stupid self!" Bracie told him.

"What do you want from Tyler? You are pushing him to the altar so fast he can't even think straight. You want him to marry you before he gets you to sign a prenuptial agreement!"

Bracie looked at Greg, "You are more stupid than I thought. You think I want this house? I will be living here, because it is where Tyler chooses to live. My one bedroom apartment was doing me fine," she said.

"You think you are slick, you tease him by not having sex with him so you got him dangling like a puppet." Greg snarled at her.

"You are crazy, it's called morals, which I see you have none of. Greg I don't know what your problem is, and I really don't care. Tyler deserves to have someone love him for the man that he is, not for the stuff that he has. He has a right to come home to a wife who loves him and will nurture him so he can have the strength to go out and do what he does so people like you can get paid."

Greg shook his head "That's a bunch of bull you don't believe yourself."

Bracie walked up on Greg until she almost touched him. With venom in her voice she told Greg, "If you ever touch me again I am going to mess you up, but if you ever hurt Tyler, I will kill you." Bracie turned to walk away.

"Don't you threaten me," Greg growled at her.

Bracie stopped and turned back to Greg. She had fire in her eyes. "No Greg, that is not a threat. If you ever do anything to hurt Tyler, I am going to kill you." She slapped him again and told him, "That's a promise!"

She left Greg standing there holding his face. He was livid.

"No woman has ever stood up to me before and that tramp has slapped me twice," he thought and left without saying anything to Tyler.

Shanelle stood there for only a second after Greg left and fell on the floor, she was laughing so hard. Tyler couldn't believe how Bracie stood up to Greg for him. He also realized he better

Bracie

not make her mad, because her right swing was nothing to mess with.

Shanelle told Tyler, "Let Bracie mention the disagreement. She's strong Tyler, and I believe she can handle her own. I do advise you to change your locks and alarm code."

Tyler agreed and saw Shanelle out.

Bracie went to her room and showered. She felt dirty where Greg tried to kiss her. "I knew he was up to no good when he brushed up against me," she thought. She sat on the bed and realized how angry she really was. Tyler knocked on the door, Bracie told him to come on in. When Tyler stepped in, she didn't bother to get up.

Tyler sat next to her, "You okay, Bracie?"

"Yes," she said.

"I heard you and Greg exchanging words; by the time I got to the kitchen he was gone."

Bracie touched Tyler's hand, "We had to get an understanding of our positions in your life. I think he was a little jealous, but he will be okay," she told him.

"Do you want me to take him out of the wedding?" Tyler asked.

"Oh no," Bracie said. "He is your friend so let him stand with you."

Tyler stood up and took Bracie's hand for her to stand up, too. He hugged her and kissed her. Tyler pulled the covers back on the bed and told her to get in. He kissed her on the cheek, turned off the light, and closed the door. Bracie was sleep by the time Tyler got in his bed. Unfortunately he did not fall asleep as quickly as Bracie did. He was trying to fathom Greg calling his wife a tramp and what did she mean, "don't' touch her again!"

Chapter Nineteen

Bracie stood in the hotel suite with her mother and Sheila.

"Are you nervous yet?" Sheila asked.

Bracie was calm, because Romesha and Shanelle had everything under control.

"Shanelle and Vanessa will be in this evening and Sondra will be in tomorrow," Bracie said to no one in particular. Bracie wanted to take a nap, but every time she closed her eyes she would see Tyler's naked body. "I have to work with all that," she thought and that made her even more nervous, because she was sure Tyler was larger than average. "Oh, I'm trippin," Bracie laughed trying to convince herself differently.

Shanelle and Vanessa arrived at the hotel and all the ladies went to one of her favorite restaurants for dinner. Bracie loved eating there; the atmosphere was perfect for small gatherings and fun. They were seated, when ten of Bracie's friends from church came in.

"Congratulations!" They had decorations, balloons, and gifts. Bracie's friends told her how gorgeous she was last Friday night.

Vanessa turned to Bracie, "Everyone in California is trying to figure out who designed your gown, it was absolutely beautiful," she said.

"Mi Madre," Bracie giggled.

"Who is that?" Vanessa asked puzzled.

Everyone was laughing. "It's my mother, in Spanish!" D'john said.

"Well girlfriend, this is your bridal shower, so let the fun begin."

They ordered their food and opened gifts while they waited.

Everyone bought lingerie and Bracie was glad. Ms. Deanie sat back and watched her daughters. Francine and Randy were by Bracie's side during the entire shower. They understood their sister would be leaving Houston to make California her home, and they wanted as much time with her as possible. As the shower winded down, Bracie asked Francine if she could squeeze Shanelle and Vanessa in to get their hair styled. Francine told them both to be at her salon by 10:00 a.m. Bracie and her bridal attendants went back to the hotel. They showered and sat around to talk. Romesha asked Bracie a question, but never got an answer because Bracie had gone to sleep.

"Well ladies, let's follow after the bride."

They turned out the lights and were all asleep in no time.

Friday was a busy day for everyone. Last minute details seemed to arrive every five minutes. Shanelle and Vanessa went to the beauty salon, while Bracie made sure Tyler's room was reserved and ready. She packed all her belongings and took them to their room. Tyler would sleep there tonight, but it's also where they would spend the first two nights of their marriage. Bracie wanted to go back to the Bahamas, and their flight would leave on Monday.

Vanessa and Shanelle were finished. They were amazed at how strong and healthy their hair looked. "Girl, what did you put in my hair?" Vanessa asked, loud as usual.

"My line of Heavenly Hair products," Francine answered.

"Is this stuff sold in California?" she asked.

"No, just locally," Francine answered her again.

"Well let me buy everything you just used on my head," Vanessa said while she primped in the mirror. "After all this is over, we will talk about getting this to California."

"Ok," Francine answered and went to her next client.

Bracie was ready to go; she was excited about seeing Tyler. She missed him.

Carl and Josh walked into the lobby with Tyler. They seemed to be engrossed in a deep discussion, until Tyler saw Bracie. He opened his arms to her as she walked swiftly to him.

"I missed you," he whispered in her ear.

"Ditto," she said as Tyler bent down to kiss her.

"We are going up for a minute. I'll meet up with you guys later." They all said okay and went to check on their rooms. Tyler knew Bracie would not have gotten the penthouse, so he was not surprised when they got out on the 10th floor. Bracie gave him the key and they went inside.

"It does have a bed." Tyler thought he whispered.

"Of course it has a bed," Bracie replied.

Tyler laughed at the look on her face. "We will be married by this time tomorrow," he said with a smile.

"I know," she said as she reached over to kiss him again. In the middle of their kiss there was a knock on the door. Bracie smiled at Tyler as she went to answer the door.

"Enough of that," Bracie's attendants teased Tyler.

Shanelle told Tyler, "She will see you tomorrow," and took Bracie back to their suite.

They all laughed and teased Bracie about her honeymoon.

Everyone went over their attire to be sure everything was in place. As the ladies started to retire, Bracie took a card out of her makeup bag and gave it to Vanessa.

"It's an encouragement card for Cherralyn."

Bracie

"How did you find the time to get her a card?" Vanessa asked.

Bracie smiled and told her, "You make the time, now let's go to bed."

It was Bracie's wedding day, and she was too excited to be nervous. All the ladies were in the suite taking pictures. After the photo shoot they all went downstairs to get ready for the wedding to begin. Ms. Deanie and her daughter were still in the suite. Temina took a few more pictures and left them alone. They gathered together and Ms. Deanie prayed for them.

Romesha stuck her head in the door, "It's time, Mama."

Meanwhile, Temina was downstairs taking pictures of Tyler and his groomsmen.

Bracie walked to the main entrance of the ballroom. Anthany stood there waiting for her. Bracie hugged her son and turned towards the door.

"You look so beautiful, Mama."

"Thank you, son," she said. The attendants opened the double doors and Bracie looked ahead to see Tyler waiting for her. She held on to Anthany and her bouquet of white roses and took her first step down the aisle.

Tyler was ready to get married. He watched as they opened the doors. He thought his heart was going to stop when Bracie stepped into the doorway. He knew at this moment God really loved him, for He sent one of his angels from heaven here to be his wife. Tears ran down his face as Bracie walked towards him. Bracie took Tyler's arm and stood before Pastor Brooks and God and repeated their vows. Bracie's hand trembled as Tyler slid her ring on. Tyler was surprised to see that the band Bracie had for him matched hers. She smiled at the look on his face. Tyler wiped her tears with the back of his hand when Oliver sang *The Lord's Prayer*.

"Tyler you may now kiss your bride," Pastor Brooks said.

Tyler knew at this moment he didn't have to be cautious anymore. He lifted her chin with one hand, pulled her close with the other, and kissed his wife for the first time.

"Oh my God, help me." Bracie thought as Tyler held on to her. When he finally let her go, Bracie felt weak. Tyler got just the reaction he wanted and smiled down at her. When Pastor Brooks introduced them as husband and wife, Bracie turned and hugged him, for he had been like a father to her since she joined the church.

When they finished taking pictures, Bracie danced with her sons to *A Song for Mama*, by Boyz II Men. When the song ended, each son kissed her on the cheek and left her on the floor for Tyler. He walked up as their song began to play, *I Found Love (Cindy's Song)*, by BeBe Winans. Tyler and Bracie danced while everyone watched and Temina took pictures.

Bracie

John looked at Bracie and felt his heart racing in his chest. "My God, she looks beautiful, and she looks so happy." He was very happy for her.

Tyler and Bracie cut the cake and made their champagne toast. Bracie threw her flower bouquet and Tyler tossed the garter. They were mingling and taking pictures when Tyler walked her over to the mike. He thanked everyone for coming out and sharing in their celebration and announced they would be leaving soon.

Bracie was standing by herself when Greg walked up to her.

"Hello Bracie, you look beautiful," he said.

"You could care less. What do you want?" she replied.

"Nothing today; enjoy your moment while you can," he sneered.

Anthany walked up, "You okay, mama?" He asked her the question, but never took his eyes off of Greg. Anthany moved between them and Greg slunk off.

"Thanks son, but I am okay," she said.

"Sure," he replied and made sure she was not alone for the rest of the evening. When Tyler and Bracie prepared to leave, she saw Anthany talking with Carl and his brothers. She turned her focus back to Tyler and her guests. She saw Dwayne talking to her mother, but she didn't have time to go and speak. The elevator opened and she and Tyler stepped in.

Chapter Twenty

When Tyler and Bracie walked into their room, she asked Tyler if he wanted to shower first.

Tyler looked at Bracie and told her, "No, we will shower later," as he was taking off his coat. Bracie stood in the middle of the floor watching Tyler as he turned the lights down and the covers back. He opened the night stand drawer and put a towel and a small bottle on top of it. She looked at him as he walked in front of her. Tyler took his wife into his arms and kissed her. Bracie kissed him back as he unbuttoned her jacket. By the time he got to the last button, his phone rang. Tyler stopped to answer it.

"Hello... what?...I'm busy, take care of it!" He turned his phone off and threw it on the chair.

Bracie had not moved, and Tyler knew exactly where he left off. He kissed her shoulders as he took the jacket off and tossed it on the chair. He started unbuttoning his shirt, but Bracie

Bracie

moved his hands. She kissed his chest as each button came undone. Bracie tossed Tyler's shirt somewhere. He ran his lips down her neck to the sensitive spot at the base of her neck and shoulder. When Tyler opened his mouth to suck her neck, Bracie squeezed him tight and let out a moan of pleasure.

"Oh Tyler," she whispered. He needed to get these clothes off of her, yet he did not want to rush this moment. Bracie pulled his undershirt over his head and kissed his chest while she rubbed her hands across his shoulders. She took her time to be sure he was enjoying her touch. Bracie undid Tyler's pants and he stepped out of everything and stood before her.

"Bracie your hands are so soft and warm." He smiled at her.

Tyler caressed the side of her face.

Tyler smiled as he watched her chew on her bottom lip. He removed her lip with his finger and kissed her. She walked over to the bed with Tyler. Bracie sat down and then lay back on the bed. Tyler went down to her feet to remove her stockings. As he started to kiss her, the phone to the room rang. Bracie could tell Tyler was annoyed now.

He picked up the receiver and answered, "WHAT?... ARE YOU SERIOUS?... look, that's what I pay you for…HANDLE IT!...Greg if you call me again for any reason… YOU'RE FIRED!" Tyler slammed the phone down in his face.

Tyler turned to Bracie and quickly forgot the phone call. He went back to kissing Bracie.

"I need to be with you, Bracie," Tyler said.

Bracie's body was on fire and soon his kisses were not enough. She lifted Tyler's head and told him softly to make love to her. She looked up at Tyler, and looked away shyly.

"Bracie, look at me." She looked into his eyes.

"Listen to my voice and hold me, Bracie." She held on to his arms.

"Now relax, baby." Tyler spoke to her softly as they slowly became one.

He knew their first time would be uncomfortable to her. He could feel her nails digging into his arms.

"Relax, Bracie," Tyler said as he bent down and started kissing her slowly over her face.

"I love you, Bracie," he said and kissed her again very passionately.

Bracie let his arms go and slid her hand behind his head to get the kiss that she wanted. He kissed her and waited for her. Bracie caressed Tyler's face and brought it down to kiss her. Tyler was doing all he could to wait for her.

"Make love to me, Tyler." Bracie said. Bracie's pain was gone and all she could feel now was the fiery pleasure Tyler was so patiently providing her.

"Let it go, Bracie, I need you baby," Tyler whispered in her ear. "Please baby," he said again.

Bracie grabbed Tyler around his shoulders. Bracie arched her back and gave in to the feelings that flowed from her body. Tyler wrapped his arms under Bracie and held her tightly.

Bracie

"Bracie, Bracie," Tyler said her name deep from within as he gave in to his pleasure. They both lay there breathing hard, their bodies were depleted of energy. Tyler lay on his back and pulled Bracie into his arms.

"I love you, Mrs. Shaw," he told her.

"I love you, Mr. Shaw," Bracie replied.

He reached over and they shared a long kissed. Bracie was sleep before Tyler's head touched his pillow.

Meanwhile downstairs, Shanelle was standing behind Greg when he hung up the phone.

"Why did you do that?" she asked.

"Do what?" Greg tried to play dumb.

"Why did you call Tyler's room with that BS?" she asked very annoyed with him.

"I needed his input on…"

"You didn't need his input on anything down here. You were purposely trying to distract him from Bracie," she cut him off.

"Shut up, Shanelle, you are not Tyler's savior." Greg said under his breath.

Shanelle looked at Greg and stepped closer to him. "Whatever your problem is with Bracie, let it go, if you don't it's going to cost you in the end."

"It sure is," Vanessa said as she walked up on them.

Greg only stared at Vanessa, he knew she was crazy and would probably fight him.

"Your horns show when Bracie is around. If you do anything to hurt her, Tyler will be the least of your worries."

"Are you threatening me, Vanessa?" Greg asked.

"You know I will take you on any day of the week," Vanessa said as she and Shanelle laughed. "If you bother her, you will have to answer to them," she pointed as all three of Bracie's sons passed by.

Greg knew he didn't want to tangle with the oldest one, but he would never say it out loud. Both ladies saw the look of fear that flashed across Greg's face, but they also knew he would not stop. They could not figure out why.

Everyone was gone from the wedding venue except Carl and Shanelle. They were taking care of finishing up the wedding and security details. They went over the checklist and headed upstairs. Once they showered and were in bed, Carl and Shanelle swapped stories about Greg.

"What is it about Bracie? I have never seen Greg act so badly towards someone Tyler cared for," Shanelle said.

Carl sat up and turned towards Shanelle. "Bracie is different. Tyler is in love with her and now he is married to her. Greg feels he has lost some power over Tyler he never really had. He feels threatened by Bracie's strength."

Bracie

"He should be," Shanelle laughed as she thought about Bracie slapping him, twice. Carl shook his head at Shanelle and then quieted her laughs with a kiss.

Tyler and Bracie slept in. When they woke up, Bracie got out of bed first and put on Tyler's shirt. He lay there and watched her move around the room. Bracie picked up her suit and folded it. She needed to get it to her mom to have it cleaned. She turned to ask Tyler a question and blushed as he continued to watch her.

"You were about to ask me something," Tyler said.

"Yes, are we going to Mama's for dinner?" she asked.

Tyler looked at the clock and pulled back the covers. When he stood up, Bracie looked at him and bit her lip. She took a deep breath and walked over to him. Tyler was going to shower, but Bracie's request to make love to her changed his mind.

By the time they finished, both of their stomachs were grumbling. They showered together, got dressed, and went for Sunday dinner.

Everyone was glad to see the couple when they arrived at Ms. Deanie's. The wedding was the main topic of the day. Bracie fixed her and Tyler a plate and sat down next to him to eat. When Tyler got up to put their plates in the sink, JeKeith walked over to his grandmother. Bracie smiled, but she got a little teary eyed. She knew it would be a while before she would see her grandson again. JeKeith gave Bracie his hand and she put his fingers to her lips as usual.

"Say grandma," she told him. JeKeith made his first attempt at saying grandma. The entire house got quiet as Bracie held his fingers and said "Grandma" once again. JeKeith looked at his grandmother with a big smile and once again tried to say grandma. Tears ran down Bracie's face as she gave him a hug. When JeKeith ran off to play, Tyler held on to Bracie as she broke down. He didn't know the story, but he knew there was a strong bond between Bracie and this grandson. Tyler and Bracie spent most of their day with Bracie's family. Leaving that evening was very emotional for they all knew after the honeymoon, Bracie would be going to California. Ms. Deanie hugged her daughter and Tyler.

"Have fun and be happy," she said.

On their way out of the door, Bracie told them she would see them in June while smiling at Trevion.

When they got to the hotel, Tyler ran Bracie a hot bath. He helped her undress and get into the tub. He lit some candles and left her to soak and unwind. Tyler could see the tears streaming down her face again. He went and sat at the table to make a few phone calls. Bracie walked out of the restroom and smiled at him.

"You okay?" Tyler teased.

Bracie assured him she would be fine, it would take some time to adjust but she would do fine in California. Tyler went to shower and Bracie sat on the bed and called John. They talked for a moment and hung up. Bracie started to put the phone down, but didn't.

"Bracie? Hey Sweetie," Dwayne said.

"Hey Biker Boy," Bracie laughed.

"I'm surprised to hear from you so soon," he said.

"Yeah, I know. I wanted to thank you for coming to the wedding."

"Thank you for inviting me, and I had to be there," he replied.

They were quiet for a moment.

"Dwayne?"

"Yes, Bracie?"

She was quiet again.

"I know, Bracie. You will always be my sweetie. Please stay in touch." Dwayne told her.

"I will and that's a promise," she told him.

"Bracie?"

"Yes, Dwayne?"

"You were a beautiful bride."

"Thank you very much. I better get off the phone now, bye Biker Boy," she said.

They both laughed and hung up. Tyler came out of the bathroom with only a towel wrapped around him. Bracie picked up his pajamas and tossed them on a chair. She stretched her arms out to him.

"Make love to me Tyler," she said softly.

Tyler let the towel fall to the floor and made love to his wife.

Carl and Shanelle were home relaxing. It had been a long weekend and everything turned out wonderfully. Carl reached over and took a ring out of its box. When Shanelle wasn't paying attention he slipped it on her finger.

"Carl what are you…?" she stopped mid sentence when she saw the ring.

"Marry me, Shanelle. I can't keep sneaking around. I love you and I want to spend the rest of my life with you."

Shanelle was speechless. She nodded yes and kissed Carl.

"What do you think Tyler will say when he finds out?" she asked.

Carl laughed at Shanelle. He's going to say congratulations."

"We both work for him, and he might not approve," she said. Carl kept laughing.

"It doesn't matter because you already said yes," he teased her.

"Carl?"

"Yes?" he answered.

"Please give me more than six weeks to plan my wedding," Shanelle said laughing.

Bracie

"You know why Tyler needed to get married so fast. He was tired of those cold showers and leaving Bracie back in Houston," he said. "Those cold showers ain't no joke," he said, while he and Shanelle cracked up.

Chapter Twenty-one

Tyler and Bracie stood at the front of their home. He unlocked the door and opened it. He turned and swept Bracie off of her feet.

"Oh Tyler," she said as he carried her into the house and closed the door.

By the time Bracie's feet touched the floor, she and Tyler were kissing.

"Umph!" Carl cleared his throat to get their attention.

Bracie and Shanelle hugged each other and went into the sitting room while Tyler and Carl carried the luggage upstairs.

Bracie told Shanelle all about their honeymoon.

"So what have you been doing while I was gone?" Bracie asked.

Shanelle showed Bracie her ring.

"It's about time," Bracie told Shanelle as she gave her a hug.

Bracie

"You're not going to ask who?"

"It better be Carl," Bracie laughed.

"How long have you known?" Shanelle asked really surprised.

"For a while now; I have seen some things," Bracie teased Shanelle.

They were still laughing and talking when the men came in. Tyler sat next to Bracie and put his arm around her. When Carl did the same to Shanelle, Tyler said, "Ok, what's going on?"

They all laughed.

Carl touched Shanelle's hand and told Tyler, "I asked Shanelle to marry me, and she said yes."

"I know we both work for you, and I hope it's okay with you," Shanelle said.

Tyler laughed at her . "You are my sister, not my employee. Come here girl." He gave her a big hug.

Tyler told Carl and Shanelle "If it is okay with Bracie and you two, I would love to host your wedding here."

All three said "Yes!" at once.

Tyler and Bracie had been home for three days and not made love. He didn't know why, but he did not want to rush her. He sat at his desk going over some of his financial sheets. Again Tyler saw something was wrong, but could not pinpoint it. He made a note and put it with the other three sets of papers. He had been preoccupied with the wedding, but now he needed to focus on his work. Tyler stepped out of the office and told Kenneth to step in.

"Have a seat," he said.

Kenneth sat down. Although he and Tyler were cool because of Sondra, he had never been called into his office before.

"You work here part time?" Tyler asked.

"Yes sir," Kenneth replied and Tyler wrote something down.

"Where else do you work?"

Kenneth told Tyler he finished college courses to become a CPA, but had not found anything full time.

"How would you like to work for me full time?" Tyler asked him.

"Why, yes sir," he said.

Tyler told him, "You start right now."

He took the papers out of the drawer and explained what he noticed. Tyler looked at Kenneth and told him, "I trust you now; if that trust remains you have a job for life. If you think the numbers will affect who you are, you can walk out the door and we will both forget we ever had this conversation."

Kenneth stood and stuck out his hand. "The trust will remain, you have my word."

Tyler took Kenneth to his new office. "I will have your name put on the door tomorrow. There are two keys to this office, and you are not to copy the one I am going to give you.

Your work is confidential, and you will share it with no one but me. Do you understand?"

"Yes sir," Kenneth answered again.

Tyler was impressed by his quick response to authority. "As long as we are in this building, it is business. Do you have a problem separating business from personal?"

"No sir, Mr. Shaw," he answered.

Tyler gave him an envelope, "Your key and your first paycheck."

Kenneth shook Tyler's hand, "Thank you sir, but today is my first day."

Tyler laughed, "I'm the boss. I can make exceptions to the rules, but you can't. Now you and Sondra go celebrate, and I will see you tomorrow morning at eight sharp."

Kenny went straight home and told Sondra what happened.

Bracie said she would talk to Tyler, and she kept her promise.

"Where is the envelope?" she asked. They opened it and they both sat down in fear of fainting. Tyler had just given Kenneth his first test in confidentiality.

Later, Tyler walked into the kitchen and tossed his keys on the counter. They hit an envelope with his name on it. It was in Bracie's handwriting. He opened it up and pulled out the note card. It read - 1 Corinthians 7:3-4 *Let the husband render unto the wife due benevolence: and likewise the wife unto the husband. The wife hath not power of her own body, but the husband: and likewise also the husband hath not power of his own body, but the wife.*

Matthew 19:5-6 *And said, For this cause shall a man leave father and mother, and shall cleave to his wife: and they twain shall be one flesh. Where they are no more twain, but one flesh. What therefore God hath joined together, let not man put asunder.* TONIGHT WE SHALL BECOME ONE. Love, Bracie Shaw.

Tyler read the card several times to be sure he was reading it correctly. He put it down and went upstairs. He opened the door to their bedroom and stood there. Bracie placed roses and candles around the room. She smiled at Tyler.

"Come and shower," she told him.

Tyler went into the bathroom and got into the shower.

Bracie lit the candles and put on *The Wedding Song* by Kenny G. She pressed the repeat button and stepped in front of the mirror. She let her ponytail down and took off her pink cotton robe. Tyler only had his blue robe set out for him, so he put it on and stepped back into the bedroom. Tyler stared at Bracie as if she were truly an angel. The white flowing spaghetti strap gown was even more beautiful than the one she had taken on their honeymoon. Bracie walked over to him and put his arms around her. Tyler kissed her as they danced by candlelight in their bedroom. Bracie took Tyler by the hand and took him to their bed and watched him get in. Bracie had pillows positioned on the bed, and Tyler leaned back against them. She leaned over his body and kissed him.

"Did you see the envelope downstairs?" she asked.

He only nodded.

"Good," she said softly.

Bracie kissed Tyler's face slowly. Tyler wanted to close his eyes, but he wanted to forever remember watching Bracie make love to him. She kissed him deeply, passionately, and slowly. Tyler followed her lead. Bracie kissed Tyler's hand and each of his fingers. She caressed Tyler's face with hers. She laid him back on the pillows.

Bracie took Tyler's hand and put it to her heart. Tyler opened his eyes and looked at her.

"Feel my heartbeat, Tyler," Bracie said softly.

Tyler relaxed his hand so he could feel Bracie's heartbeat.

She placed her hand on his heart and told him, "Become one with me, Tyler."

Bracie put her hand on top of Tyler's as tears ran down her face.

Tyler reached over to kiss Bracie's tears as they mingled with his own. When Bracie called his name, he knew he had her heart. Tyler was so full he was shaking. For the first time in his life he felt God was in his bedroom. He knew what just happened had nothing to do with sex. Tyler lifted Bracie's face and looked into her eyes.

"I love you Bracie; I am so in love with you." He held her close to him for awhile.

Tyler sat Bracie up and got out of bed. She watched as he blew out each candle and turned off the stereo. Tyler picked up a single rose and brought it to bed with them. He rubbed it across her face. Bracie pulled Tyler's face close to hers. He smiled and this time he took the lead.

Carl had been waiting for Tyler since seven that morning. It was not like him to be late. Tyler walked into the kitchen and tried to pour a cup of coffee.

"What's wrong, why are you shaking?" Carl asked. Tyler knew he could trust Carl.

"It's Bracie."

Carl didn't say anything, he just let Tyler talk.

"Last night ... I have never experienced anything like that before." Tyler looked over at Carl

"It was like she made love to me from her soul. It felt like God was in the room with us, man! I wanted to pull her inside of me and hold her there. I love her Carl. I can't be without her. Ever."

Carl touched Tyler on the shoulder while he stood there trying to get himself together.

"You have never experienced love like that before, because you have never been married to her before. She feels free to love you now Tyler; you are her husband."

"Wise beyond your years," Tyler told Carl as they left for the studio.

Bracie didn't get up until after nine. She turned over and hugged Tyler's pillow so she could smell his scent. Tyler didn't know how loving and passionate he could be until last night. Bracie knew he understood their love, when he put his hand back to her heart. She smiled as she turned over to get out of bed.

"Ok, Bracie. It is time for you to start making a life for yourself here in California," she said to herself as she headed for the shower.

Once Bracie got dressed she went downstairs into her office. She stood in the doorway to look at how beautiful it was. "Thank you Father," she said and sat behind her desk. Bracie pulled out her blueprints for The Master's Peace. She went through some of her poetry and book ideas for hours before she realized she had not eaten. She left everything as it was and went to cook dinner for her husband.

Chapter Twenty-two

Bracie took her first trip back to Houston as Mrs. Shaw. She knocked on Dianne's door. She missed her neighbor. She saw her at the wedding, but never got a chance to talk with her.

Dianne opened the door, "Hey Bracie, how have you been, how was your honeymoon, where did you go, how are you?" She went on until Bracie stopped her. They both laughed!

"Do you have time for lunch?" Bracie asked her.

"Sure, let me get my purse." Dianne and Bracie ate lunch at Hicks Barbeque. Bracie spoke to her nephews Terry and Steven as she entered the restaurant. She and Dianne laughed and talked as Dianne gave Bracie a rundown of everything that happened since she has been gone. Dianne slightly pushed Bracie's shoulder.

"What?" Bracie said laughing.

"I knew that was Tyler Shaw leaving your apartment that day," she said.

Bracie

Bracie smiled at the look on her face. Dianne had a puzzled look on her face now.

"What's the matter?" Bracie asked.

Dianne dropped her head. "Bracie I know this is personal, but..."

Bracie already knew what was on her mind. It was one of the reasons she came to see her neighbor.

"No Dianne, I did not sleep with Tyler until we were married."

Dianne lifted her head, "But I saw him leave your apartment early in the morning several times."

Bracie just looked at Dianne. "You've been arguing with some of those busybodies at the apartment, haven't you?"

Dianne laughed and said, "Yes!"

Bracie hugged her. "I'm sorry I put you in such a bad position, Dianne. You have my word as a friend that I did not have sex with Tyler until our wedding night."

Dianne's happy go lucky mood returned. She went on about her neighbors. They enjoyed their time together and Bracie took Dianne home. She made sure to wave at a few of the ladies as they drove in. Dianne didn't tell Bracie these ladies teased her by saying Bracie didn't really like her and would forget her. Bracie parked and they got out. She picked up a bag off the back seat and gave it to Dianne.

"I picked it out for you while on my honeymoon. I hope you like it."

Dianne took the angel out of the bag. It was engraved "Friends Forever, Love Bracie."

"Thank you Bracie, I'll miss you." Dianne hugged her.

"Thank you for believing in me enough to stand up for me," Bracie said "I promise to stay in touch." Bracie got in her car and went to her mother's.

Everyone met at Andre' and D'john's for Trevion's graduation celebration. Family gatherings, this was a part of her life at home in Houston that she would miss. Bracie made a toast and presented him with a $1,000 gift card to decorate his dorm. Everyone laughed when she gave the card to his parents. Ms. Deanie gave a toast and presented him with the leather jacket he had been eyeing since the winter. After that, everyone went back to partying. Bracie looked up as John walked into the house. They hugged each other and he kissed her on top of her head.

"I remember you crying on my shoulder when you found out D'john was pregnant with this boy and now he is graduating!"

"I must have been a terrible sight," Bracie said.

When John said yes, they both started laughing.

Francine walked over to her sister, "How is life in California so far?"

"It's good, can't complain yet," they both laughed.

Francine told Bracie Vanessa had kept her word. They finalized selling her Heavenly Hair products in California.

"Bracie, she didn't want any profit. Vanessa said she helped me because you helped her. She didn't say how you helped her, she just said you did."

Bracie smiled and wondered, helped her how?

Tyler and Bracie talked on the phone for a few hours before she went to bed, but she still woke up early feeling refreshed. She went into the kitchen to have coffee with her mom.

"Good morning Mama." She kissed Ms. Deanie on the cheek. She sat down and they talked for awhile. It was soon time to get dressed so Bracie rinsed their cups and put them in the sink. Most of her family met her outside of the TSU auditorium. Bracie was caught off guard by the press. They were snapping pictures and asking questions. It took her a moment to get herself together. Bracie stood tall and asked them to stop taking her picture.

"Look I don't want to be rude. I know being married to Tyler Shaw has some paparazzi drawbacks, but today is about my oldest grandson graduating high school. Please don't make this about me, because it won't be fair to him."

Bracie's family and friends surrounded her so the press couldn't reach her again. For the most part they respected her wishes and backed off, but they still printed what they had taken.

Bracie was glad to see all of her friends, and she was beginning to miss her home church already. The adjustment was going to be harder than she thought. Bracie spent time with Shani and took plenty of pictures with her and Sheila. They all ate dinner at Ms. Deanie's. Bracie stepped out on the porch, and Randy followed her.

"What's up, sis?" she asked.

Bracie tried to smile and say nothing, but it wouldn't come out. By that time D'john, Romesha, and Francine came outside, too. They gave Bracie a group hug,

"We know it's hard sis, but you have a wonderful husband and new friends there."

"I know," Bracie said "I will be okay." "If it will make you feel better, invite us out there one weekend, and we can celebrate," they said jokingly.

Bracie dried her tears and enjoyed being with her family. Bracie went to bed early, she would miss her family, but right now she was missing Tyler.

Chapter Twenty-three

Tyler had already gone to the studio when Carl picked Bracie up from the airport.

"Can you wait until I change?" she asked Carl.

He pulled up and took her luggage upstairs. Bracie already knew what she was going to put on so it didn't take long.

"Where to Ms. Bracie?" he asked.

"The studio, I want to see my husband."

Carl smiled and drove her to the studio.

"I don't know my way around. Can you get me to Tyler?"

"Sure," and he took her where Tyler should be.

"Are they filming, is it okay to see him?" she asked Shanelle while giving her a hug.

Tyler was talking to the crew, giving out directions on how to set up for the next shoot. Bracie looked around, "This place is huge and I have no idea of how I got in here," she thought.

Tyler saw her standing with Shanelle.

"Take ten," he said and walked over towards Bracie.

Ten minutes would pass quickly so Bracie looked for something to hold. She asked Shanelle for a stack of folders sitting on a table and held the folders in front of her. Bracie smiled broadly. Shanelle knew Bracie was up to something she just didn't know what.

Tyler came over and talked for a minute.

"Hey Angel," he said while giving her a hug.

"Tyler, will you reach into my pocket and get the card I have for you?" Bracie said it with a huge smile on her face. Tyler stepped behind Bracie and stuck his hand in her pocket.

"Bracie," he whispered in her ear. Tyler pulled Bracie closer to him and stuck his hands further into her pants where her pockets used to be. She stepped away. She gave Shanelle back the folders and told Tyler she would see him at home.

"Bye, Ms. Bracie," the crew waved to her.

Before she could answer back, Tyler grabbed her hand and yelled to the crew, "Go over your orders, I'm through for the day!"

Carl, Shanelle, and Kenneth turned to ask Tyler a question. He cut them off.

"I have something in my office I need to take care of, and Carl, Bracie will be riding home with me." They all stood there confused. What was that all about? No one had any idea so they went back to work.

Tyler pulled Bracie into his office and locked the door. He kissed her hard. Bracie was pinned against the door.

"Tyler!" she cried out.

"Bracie!"

"Tyler, are you okay?" Bracie asked.

"Yeah, except you're trying to kill me," he teased.

They were both laughing until someone knocked on the door.

"Mr. Tyler, we are shutting down for the evening; we will see you tomorrow."

"Okay!" he replied to whoever was on the other side of the door.

Bracie lay in Tyler's arms until they could breathe again.

"I missed you, Bracie."

"I missed you, too," Bracie said as she sat up and looked at Tyler.

"What's on your mind, Angel?" he asked.

"Just now, I have never been that free before, I mean."

Tyler sat up in front of Bracie and put his finger on her lips. "It's what you wanted, it's what you needed. Thank you, Jesus!," he said teasing her. "No, baby for real, it's a part of life. If you had not shown me what you meant, I would not have known what to do or rather how to do it."

Bracie laughed, "So when I want something from you, that's all I need to do?"

"You betcha!" Tyler said as they laughed again. He touched Bracie's face.

Tyler kissed Bracie, "Now let me show you what I want."

Greg had been standing behind one of the props. He was still trying to figure out what Tyler had taken out of Bracie's pocket. *"She is making this hard for me."* He could hear her calling Tyler's name. Tyler didn't allow any improprieties on the premises or anywhere associated with T. Wahs Production; it was not tolerated. They lost several good crewmen because of it. She has this fool breaking his own rules, he thought. *"Use your head Greg, you have to get rid of her before she takes everything you have worked for."* He stayed two hours after everyone left, and they were still locked up in Tyler's office.

Angela knew he was upset the moment he stepped inside.

"Hello Greg," she said. He looked at her and spoke rather nicely. He gave her a hug and a kiss. They sat down for dinner and enjoyed a glass of wine after. Angela knew why he was so nice as soon as they got into bed. He needed someone to release all of his frustrations into. She lay there wondering why was she taking this? Greg had not made love to her in a long time, then she thought about it, he had never made love to her. Greg rolled over and turned his back to her. Angela knew it was time for her change to come.

Bracie sat on the sofa next to Tyler.

Bracie

"Baby, will it be okay for me to invite my mom and daughters down for the July fourth weekend?"

Tyler turned towards Bracie. "Of course you can! This is your home now. You don't have to ask for our family to visit."

"I know this is my home. I ask out of respect to you as my husband and head of our household, that's all baby."

Tyler looked at her again. "You are serious about what you just said," he stated more than asked a question.

"Yes baby, I am. I will not make any major decisions for our home without passing it by you first." Tyler knew at that moment he would give up everything he had just to be with her. I have a great lover, a great cook, a woman who loves God, and respects me as the head. He felt blessed.

Tyler hugged Bracie, "Invite them all if you want. Tell them twenty tickets will be paid for on whatever airline they choose. I need you to hurry and find out so I can set it up ASAP." Bracie hugged Tyler.

"Thank you," she said as she ran to get her phone to call her mother. Bracie looked forward to having her family out to her home. She stopped by the kitchen on her way upstairs.

When Tyler came into the bedroom, he knew his wife was up to something, and he also knew it was something good.

"Come here," Bracie called out to him. Tyler walked into the room and smiled at Bracie as she sat in the middle of the bed.

The room was lit by candles only and soft jazz was playing on the stereo. Tyler had acquired Bracie's taste for non-alcoholic champagne. Tyler sat on the bed and leaned back against the headboard. Tyler put his hand in Bracie's back and pulled her to him. Tyler and Bracie sat in candlelit room listening to the music.

Tyler kissed Bracie on the back of her head

"Thank you, Bracie."

"For what?" she said teasing.

"For making me wait," Tyler said seriously.

Bracie sat up and turned to look at him. "I don't know what to say," she said.

"I understand now that you could not fully give yourself to me until we were married."

Tyler put his hand over her heart. "We are one now, Bracie. I believe God has blessed us because we were obedient. I realized I had never made love until I made love with you." Bracie sat there with tears in her eyes.

"I almost lost you, Tyler," she whispered.

"See that's where you are wrong. I was trying to give you time to get yourself together. I knew already that I loved you from my soul. What I felt for you was from God. I wasn't going anywhere."

Bracie smiled.

Tyler caressed her face. "Do you know you are the only woman who has ever told me no? I mean for anything. Bracie.

Bracie

The others wanted my money and my things more than they wanted my respect. I knew I didn't want a woman who thought so little of herself she would sell herself for things, that's all this stuff is Bracie, just things. I love you, what God has put in my heart for you I can't even explain."

Bracie still could not say anything.

"Do you know when I realized I wanted to be in your life?"

Bracie shook her head no.

"Christmas Eve, when you tried to slide out of bed without me knowing it."

They both laughed.

"Yeah, I remember that," she said.

"Truth, honesty, morals, integrity, and your love for God. I saw it all in you Bracie from our first date, and you never even realized how much it showed."

Bracie was quiet for several minutes. She appreciated so much how well he expressed how he felt about her. She loved him so much.

"Thank you, Tyler," she told him when she was finally able to talk.

"No, thank you, Bracie."

Tyler showed Bracie that night exactly what he meant and what he felt for her.

Chapter Twenty-four

Carl and Shanelle were at Bracie's house working on their wedding plans. Bracie and Vanessa would stand with her, and Tyler and Carl's brother Jason would stand with him as his best men. Angela and Sondra would be hostesses. Bracie did not trust anyone else to welcome people into her home. Carl and Shanelle set their wedding date for July sixteenth. When they finished, Bracie invited them all over for the fourth of July to spend time with her family.

"How many are coming?" asked Shanelle.

"Around twenty and they are all staying here. We have enough room to house everybody," Bracie said excitedly.

Bracie stayed home while Carl and Tyler went to pick her family up from the airport. She was standing at the front door when they pulled in. Bracie ran to Tyler's car to see her mom.

Bracie

"Bracie, you can let her go, she is coming into the house." Tyler said jokingly. Bracie's family stood outside looking at the house and gardens around them.

"Wow!" the grandkids kept saying.

Once everyone was inside, Bracie told them which room they would occupy for the weekend. "I put numbers on each door to make it easier," she said. "All the young men and boys follow me," she said. They walked out back passed the pool and into the guest house. Trevion you are the oldest, you are in charge. Whoever does not behave call me, and they will sleep inside. Tyler will be out later to give you the rules for out here."

"We have rules?" they pretended to pout.

"As long as I'm your grandma, you will always have rules."

Bracie laughed as she went back inside. She showed the ladies around while Tyler hung out with the men.

"Because you are family, I can show you the master bedroom," Bracie said on their tour of the house. She opened the double doors and let them in. They all stood inside the door speechless at its size and beauty. Necia ran straight to the bed and picked up Bracie's doll.

"Your bed is huge," D'john said while elbowing her sisters-in-law. Bracie laughed at her daughters, "Remember Tyler is over six feet tall and wait until you see the tub." Ms. Deanie watched Bracie show her home in pride. She was shocked Bracie let them into her bedroom. Bracie believed the master bedroom was always off limit to visitors. That's where a husband and wife spend their most intimate times and make their greatest decisions and you don't want crazy spirits in there, she always said. Bracie taught that to her daughter and her daughters-in-law.

Everyone met outside in the backyard garden for dinner and fun. The time went by fast and the ladies were off to bed by midnight. Tyler came up, showered, and finally crawled into bed about two that morning. As soon as he lay down Bracie instantly moved into his arms. Since they had guests in the house, they both slept in nightclothes and were too tired to let it bother them.

The women were downstairs cooking early the next morning. The smell of coffee and bacon woke the men up. Tyler stood in the doorway watching Bracie with her mom and daughters. She was happy, and it showed on her face; he could hear it in her laugh.

"Hey, I found someone about to ring the buzzer, so I brought them with me," Shanelle said as she walked in with Francine and Allen. Bracie's face lit up. Francine joined the women in the kitchen while Tyler took Allen to the sitting room with the men. Everyone gathered in the formal dining room for breakfast. Tyler blessed the food and no one moved until every dish, platter, and bowl was empty.

Bracie

The ladies had as much fun cleaning up as they did cooking. Tyler and Shanelle stood in amazement at the unity of such a large family.

"Fish fry starts at five, until then have fun!" Bracie called out to her family.

Vanessa's sons came to pick up Trevion and Le'Andre. The younger boys made use of the backyard. Je'Keith stayed close to Bracie.

"He has grown up so fast since I've been gone," Bracie said. Je'Keith saw a free ball and finally went to play. The ladies sat in the garden and enjoyed listening to Vanessa and Shanelle tell their California stories. Bracie noticed Romesha and D'john giggling among themselves.

"What are you two up too?" she asked. "Have you tried the pocket trick on Tyler?" they asked. Sondra and Vanessa looked puzzled, but Shanelle wanted to know what happened with Tyler and Bracie.

"What is that?" Vanessa asked.

Bracie didn't say anything as they explained. Shanelle turned and looked at Bracie and started laughing.

"Be quiet, Shanelle," Bracie told her laughing also.

Shanelle told everyone how Bracie's joke backfired and Tyler took her into his office. They all laughed at Bracie when she blushed at the thought of that day.

"Have you tried the restaurant trick yet?"

"No!" Bracie said, "That is coming."

Once again Romesha and D'john had to explain something out of Bracie's barrel of surprises.

Bracie was in the midst of her family for three days, and she enjoyed every minute. They were packing up the van when Tyler and Anthany went into his office. After a few minutes, Tyler opened the door and asked Carl to come inside. Bracie saw the look on his face and became concerned. They stayed in the office for over an hour. When they came out, the frown was gone from Tyler's brow. Everyone was in the van and ready to go. Bracie and her children were having a hard time saying goodbye. Bracie walked away from the van when D'john and Necia started crying. She went to the car and gave her mom a hug.

"I love you," she waved to her family as they pulled out of the driveway.

Bracie was dressed for bed and sitting at her vanity when Tyler got back. Tyler went to shower. When he came out of the bathroom, he took Bracie in his arms and kissed her.

"Has Greg said or done anything to you?" he asked.

"No, but I don't trust him," she answered. "I really think he was jealous of the time we were spending together and the fact that you didn't tell him about us. I think he's okay now."

Tyler and Bracie got into bed. She sat up and pulled her gown off.

Bracie

"I don't need this anymore," she said with a smile.

"Well I guess I don't need these either," Tyler said as he took off his pajamas and pulled Bracie into his arms.

Tyler, Greg, and Shanelle were at the studio when the call came in from New Orleans. Tyler's grandmother passed. Tyler called Carl and told him to pick up Bracie as soon as possible and meet them at the airport. Bracie had their bags packed by the time Carl got there. They boarded his plane and Bracie went to sit next to her husband and hold his hand. She stayed by his side the entire time they were in New Orleans. Bracie did not say much, but she was his shoulder to lean on and his strength. When the pallbearers slid his grandmother's casket into the vault, Tyler broke down. Larry, Josh, and Kenny came to Bracie's aid. Greg was scared to take a step towards her, because Anthany stood by her side. The ladies stood by as Carl held on to Shanelle as her tears flowed freely down her face. Anthany held his mother's hand as she watched her husband in so much pain. Bracie only met his grandmother a few times, and she was always very nice. Bracie thought about their last visit.

"Bracie, Tyler loves you; he is happy now. He had a good upbringing, but he needs to get back into the church. I'm leaving that up to you. You are good for him Bracie; keep loving my boy," she told Bracie while patting her on the back of her hand.

"Yes ma'am," Bracie promised her.

Tyler signed the house over to his cousin who grew up with him like a sister.

"Mama would want you to have the house," he told Cynthia. "If you need anything call me or Bracie," he told her.

"Mama wanted to live to see us both married and settled, so she died happy, Tyler. She died happy." Cynthia broke down again. Tyler held her and let her cry.

Tyler and Bracie slept in his grandmother's bed. She lay in Tyler's arms, held him, and prayed for him.

They all boarded the plane to go back to California. Once the plane took off, Tyler got up and went into the small conference room. Bracie asked Shanelle how to get there, because she needed to be with Tyler. Shanelle and Carl sat quietly together. She lay her head on Carl and cried herself to sleep. Greg and Kenny didn't say much to each other. Soon Kenny dozed off, too. Greg got up to go check on Tyler; he didn't go in, he stood there with the door cracked.

Bracie walked in and sat next to Tyler.

"Thank you for being here with me, Bracie," Tyler told her.

She moved and kneeled in front of him.

"This is where I belong," she said.

Tyler caressed Bracie's face and kissed her. "I need you Bracie."

That's all he needed to say to her.

Bracie

"Oh, Bracie I love you." Tyler kept saying as she held him to ease his pain.

"Kiss me, Tyler," Bracie whispered.

He lifted his head to share a long passionate kiss with her. Tyler reached up and let her hair down. Bracie pulled Tyler to her and put his head on her chest. Tyler wrapped his arms around her.

"Love me, Bracie, please baby,"

Tyler's pain began to come out. "Love me through this pain, Bracie," he said crying. Tyler tightened his hold on her, but Bracie did not let go.

"I need you, baby."

Bracie held Tyler and cried with him. She turned in time to see Greg close the door. Bracie did not say anything; she put her focus back on her husband. Tyler lay back on the seat and Bracie lay next to him. Some time had gone by when Bracie looked at the clock and knew they would be landing soon. Bracie wouldn't look Greg's way, she just held on to Tyler. But Greg could not take his eyes off of her. Tyler, Bracie, and Shanelle got into the limo, while Greg left with another woman. No one said anything, because at the moment no one cared. Tyler offered Carl and Shanelle one of the guest rooms for the night, they accepted and went upstairs. Tyler and Bracie went to their bedroom, showered and went to bed.

Chapter Twenty-five

Everything was well with Bracie and Tyler. Carl and Shanelle got married and went on a cruise for their honeymoon. Tyler and Bracie took a week's trip to celebrate their birthdays out of the country. Tyler was now preparing the production crew to film on site for three weeks in Florida. His love of Bracie seemed to be contagious to everyone except Greg. He knew he had to make his move on Tyler because he was unsuspecting of anything. Greg kept thinking about seeing them on the plane. Now he understood why Tyler wanted her. Florida would be it, Bracie would lose once and for all. He had found Tyler's weakness. "I always win," Greg said laughing.

Tyler kissed Bracie goodbye. "I'll be in Houston for a week," she told him.

"Okay, tell everyone I said hello and have fun, that's an order!" Bracie laughed at her husband as she closed the door.

She was already packed and ready to go. Carl took her to the airport and dropped her off at the loading gate.

"Have fun," he said and drove off.

While in Houston, Bracie made her rounds visiting. She talked to her nieces and nephews. She visited Steven's Barber Shop and Hicks Barbeque to see Terry and his family. She went to visit John and his mother. Bracie spent one day visiting Sheila and Shani and had dinner that same evening with Dianne. Bracie had one more person she needed to see before she left Houston. She texted Dwayne and they agreed to meet for dinner. Bracie and Dwayne hugged each other and sat down to their table.

"You look beautiful, Bracie," he said.

"Thank you."

"How is life in California?" he asked.

"It's wonderful," she answered. Bracie told him about her family visiting for the Fourth, Tyler's grandmother passing the same week, and she thanked him for the birthday card.

"You are welcome, sweetie," he told her.

Bracie smiled at him. She told Dwayne her plans for the Master's Peace and how she enjoyed working at the youth center with Vanessa twice a month. They enjoyed their dinner and time together. Dwayne and Bracie said their goodbyes. They hugged and once again promised to stay in touch.

Bracie stayed longer than a week. She enjoyed herself, but she needed to go home to greet her husband. He would be home in four days. In Florida, Tyler told the cast and crew that if everything went well, they should be through in two days instead of four so they could go home. They teased him about trying to get home to Ms. Bracie. Tyler laughed with them, because he knew they were right. He went to his hotel room and called Bracie. They talked for a short while and got off the phone. He lay back on the bed and thought about the first time they made love in their bed. He put his hand over his heart. "I feel you Bracie, I love you so much." He fell asleep with his hand over his heart.

Filming went better than expected and they finished in two days as Tyler said.

"Okay everyone, that's a wrap! If you are flying out with us, be downstairs by ten in the morning, if not I will see you Tuesday." Tyler got off the elevator happy. This time tomorrow he would be with his wife. He opened the door to his room and stepped back out to check the number. He opened the door again. In his bed was a beautiful naked woman. He looked around, stepped in, and closed the door. Greg was hiding to make sure Tyler would go in.

"Yes!" he shouted. Greg whistled as he went into his room. Angela saw it all and could not believe Tyler would cheat on Bracie. She left and went to the lobby.

Tyler was downstairs the next morning, ready to go. Only a few of the crew flew on the plane with Tyler and Shanelle. By

Bracie

the time it landed, Kenneth called Tyler and told him he needed to see him ASAP.

"Meet me at the house this evening," Tyler told him. That would give him time to get home and see his wife. Tyler was talking with Bracie when the gate buzzer rang. He left the kitchen and went to the door. Kenny went into the sitting room with Tyler.

"Where is Bracie?" Kenny asked.

"She went upstairs, now what's up?" he asked.

Shanelle walked in, "What's up, Tyler?"

"We are about to find out," Tyler said.

Kenneth laid the financial reports on the table for Tyler. He explained everything he had circled for the last three years. "Tyler, Greg has been embezzling money from you."

Tyler looked at Kenny in disbelief.

"He had you sign over your vacation home in Aspen, and you have signed papers giving him permission to access T. Wahs' overseas account."

"Are you serious?" Shanelle sat down, "I knew he was up to something, but I never thought it would be to this magnitude," she said.

Bracie was getting ready to step out of her office when Tyler started talking. "Last night when I got to my room, I had a naked guest waiting for me."

"What!" Shanelle shouted.

227

Tyler shook his head, "I need to know who got her through security and who let her in my room," he said.

"Who was she?" Kenny asked.

"I don't know, all I do know is she was naked and waiting for me in my room, in my bed." Tyler's head was down when Bracie stepped out of her office and overhears him.

Shanelle and Kenneth couldn't say or do anything as Tyler kept talking.

"Do you know what that would do to Bracie if she found out?" Tyler looked up and saw tears streaming down Shanelle's face. She looked as if she had seen a ghost. Instantly Tyler knew Bracie was standing behind him.

"Bracie, wait!" Tyler said as he stepped in and then over the sofa.

"Don't touch me! You were with some whore, Tyler? You slept with a whore you didn't even know?" Bracie screamed at him. "How could you? I trusted you Tyler. I gave you all of me and you slept with that tramp last night and then made love with me today like nothing happened!" Bracie was crying so hard she backed into the door of her office.

Tyler reached out to touch her and Bracie slapped him so hard they both stumbled. Tyler got his balanced and looked at her. Bracie stood up and slumped her shoulders.

She looked up at Tyler, "You promised you would never hurt me, and I trusted you," she said softly. The pain seemed to have drained the life out of Bracie.

Bracie

"Angel, wait." When Tyler touched Bracie again she didn't fight anymore. Without looking up she simply told him, "I trusted you."

Bracie bowed her head and told Tyler softly, "Please let me go."

"Bracie let me explain," Tyler tried to tell her.

Bracie gently took his hand off of her and went upstairs.

Tyler went into an instant rage. Shanelle stepped back because she had never seen him so angry.

"I didn't sleep with that whore, but I sure need to find out who put her there! Who in hell had the key to my room?" Tyler walked back and forth angry, mad, and pissed!

Carl came to pick up Shanelle and walked in on Tyler's rage. Carl walked up to Tyler after Shanelle explained everything to him.

"Tyler, calm down so you can think," he said.

Tyler kept pacing the room. "You didn't see the pain in her eyes. Oh God help me."

He looked at Carl.

"I told that woman to get dressed and get out. She didn't know the guy that let her in, but he gave her $5,000. She said the man found her. I told her if she ever mentioned this to anyone I would have her put under the prison for trespassing. Who would do this and why?" Tyler said.

The men stayed downstairs with Tyler, while Shanelle went upstairs to comfort Bracie. She was headed for their bedroom when she heard Bracie crying in the other room. Shanelle sat next to her. Bracie started sobbing all over again.

"I trusted him, Shanelle. I love Tyler, and I trusted him." Shanelle didn't try to explain Tyler's story or give her any advice, she just let Bracie cry. Shanelle sat with Bracie until she fell asleep. Tyler came into the room.

"Kenny is gone; lock up on your way out."

Shanelle nodded, "Good luck, brother," she said.

He gave her a crooked smile, "I'm going to need it," he said.

Tyler picked Bracie up and carried her into their bedroom. He put her in the bed and covered her up. Tyler couldn't sleep, he just sat there and watched Bracie as she cried in her sleep. He could tell her eyes were swollen even while she was still asleep. Bracie turned to sit up. She barely opened her eyes when last night came flooding back upon her. Fresh tears ran down her face. Tyler went and sat in front of her.

"Bracie, look at me." Tyler spoke softly to her. He lifted her chin. "Angel, I love you. Bracie, I promise, I did not sleep with her. You know I don't pack condoms, I don't pack them because I don't need them," Tyler said, "Bracie please stop crying." Tyler didn't know what else to say. He took her hand and put it to his heart.

"We are one, Bracie. I cannot cheat on you; you are of me, Bracie."

Bracie

She finally lifted her head. "Why was she there Tyler, who put her there?" Bracie asked through tears.

"I don't know baby, that's what I was trying to explain to Kenny and Shanelle. Somebody let her get through security and I'm going to find out who, she could have been crazy or set me up to be robbed, anything."

Bracie shook her head. "I am so sorry I hit you, Tyler."

Bracie's handprint was still on his face. He rubbed it.

"Yeah, you slapped me pretty good," he laughed.

"You wanna slap me back?" she asked giggling.

"Oh no, then I would have to answer to Anthany cause his mama detector would go off for sure." They both laughed and Tyler was so glad to see her smile again.

Tyler touched Bracie's face "I promise I will never cheat on you or hurt you Bracie. I can't, if I hurt you, then I hurt me." She nodded and lay back on the pillows while Tyler put a cold pack on her eyes. Bracie went to sleep and Tyler went downstairs to use the phone. It was late afternoon when Bracie woke up. Tyler took her to sit outside in the garden. Bracie rested her head on Tyler. She had mistaken his quietness for calmness, inside Tyler felt like a raging bull

.

Chapter Twenty-six

Tyler did not leave Bracie's side for two days. She was quiet most of the time, but Tyler knew she was okay. They had not made love since Bracie overheard him talking. Tyler needed her, but did not want to seem impatient. The more Tyler wanted to make love to Bracie, the angrier he became. Her hand print was finally gone from his face, but the pain that was on hers was still in Tyler's mind. Bracie lay in Tyler's arms that night, quiet as usual. She sat up and looked at him.

"What's wrong, Angel?" he asked.

"Are you ready to make love? I know…" Before she could go on Tyler kissed her.

"I love you, Bracie," Tyler said as he laid her back on the bed. "Thank you Father," Tyler said to himself. He reached over, turned out the lights, and made love to his wife.

Bracie

The couple was enjoying a quiet evening when Carl and Shanelle came in.

"What's up?" they asked.

"We're enjoying a movie," Tyler replied.

"Angela called and said to meet you here at seven."

"No one called us," Tyler looked at Bracie and she shook her head no. The gate buzzer went off and Tyler got up. He came back with Angela and Kenny. She spoke and went straight to the reason she asked them to meet her.

"I am leaving Greg. He has been cheating, but that's not why I am here. Tyler, Greg has been stealing from you for years. The year you bought the plane, Greg embezzled $100,000 from you."

Tyler sat up in shock. Angela didn't look at him; she gave Kenny an envelope and kept talking. "He has charged jewelry, dinners, and trips on the studio account."

She gave Kenny another envelope. She had one more in her hand that she kept fidgeting with as she continued to talk. Greg somehow got Jasmine, Shamia, and Krystalyn to sleep with him. Once they did, he blackmailed them to leave you so you wouldn't find out."

Angela took a deep breath and turned to Bracie.

"Bracie, Tyler did not cheat on you. I saw Greg let that woman in, and I saw Tyler when he went into the room. By the time I got to the lobby, she was rushing out. I caught her and told her I was head of security, and I saw a man pay her to go into Mr. Shaw's room."

Tears began to fall down Angela's face.

"Greg gave her $5,000 to sleep with Tyler, but promised to give her $10,000 more if she could get him to sleep with her unprotected because he already knew she was HIV positive. That's why she was chosen for the job."

Bracie and Shanelle covered their mouths in disbelief.

"He wanted to get rid of Bracie because she was in the way of him getting what he believed to be his, T. Wahs Production and everything that comes with it. That's why he came on to her and when that didn't work, he hated Bracie. He couldn't do anything to her because he was scared of one of her sons."

"Anthany," everyone said.

Tyler moved to the end of the sofa and touched Angela's hand.

"Half of the studio was his. Bracie has made it clear she doesn't want any of this, not even the house. It was all going to be his." Tyler looked at her, "Angela, Greg paid someone to infect me, so I could pass it to my wife, so he could have this, is that what you just said?"

She only nodded.

"What s in the other envelope?" Kenny asked.

Angela continued to look at Tyler.

"When Greg had the DNA done on Brianne, he knew it wasn't yours, but he never figured she would be his." She gave the envelope to Tyler.

"He's been paying child support since he found out."

Tyler's hands were shaking when he pulled the papers out and read them. It was all there in black and white. Tyler dropped his head and Bracie could see tears falling.

"All these years I have trusted him and treated him like a brother," he said.

Bracie got up, hugged Angela, and walked her to the door.

"Thank you for bringing this to us, but Greg will be furious with you."

Angela smirked, "Greg is stupid. I told him a long time ago to stop messing in Tyler's affairs. After Florida, he had to be stopped. My cousin is outside. We are going to Atlanta and then I'm going home. Shanelle looked at Angela puzzled.

"I have family and friends in Atlanta, but West Virginia is home. Please don't tell Greg," she said.

"Never!" Shanelle and Bracie said. They hugged Angela again and walked back inside.

When Bracie walked into the sitting room, Tyler sat there with the envelope in front of him. Bracie kneeled in front of him and put all the papers back inside. She didn't say anything, she just turned and wrapped her arms around him. Tyler held on to her tight. The room was quiet for a long time. Shanelle, Carl, and Kenny encircled the couple and Carl prayed over them.

Bracie said "Thank you," while Tyler only nodded. They sat there and Tyler stood up. When he walked around the table, he had a look on his face neither had seen before and after tonight they hoped to never see it again.

"Greg has gone too far. He has been stealing from me, and he has betrayed me. He touched my wife and tried to make a pass at her. He caused unnecessary pain in my marriage and for that he will pay," Tyler said with venom in his voice. He turned to the three people closest to him. "None of this is to leave this room. Kenny I'm sorry, but I have to ask you not to share this with Sondra."

"Yes sir," he said.

"Greg will pay!" Tyler said.

He turned and looked at Bracie, "I'm going upstairs." He turned and walked away.

Kenny picked up the two financial envelopes and left. Bracie was still standing in the same spot. She was in shock. Shanelle and Carl walked over to her.

"You okay?" they asked.

Bracie did not answer. "I need to see you out; I need to check on my husband," Bracie said in barely a whisper.

Carl and Shanelle left and Bracie went upstairs to be with her husband.

Bracie

Tyler was sitting on side of the bed with a blank look on his face. Bracie crawled in bed behind him and massaged his shoulders.

He turned and looked at Bracie. This time she didn't need to say the words, she just nodded her head yes. Tyler held and kissed Bracie so hard she thought her face would break. Then he put his head on Bracie's chest and listened to her heartbeat.

"Thank you God for my wife, my Angel," Tyler prayed quietly. When he realized he was dozing off, Tyler moved to his side of the bed and brought Bracie into his arms. Bracie lay there, but sleep would not come. When she knew Tyler was deep in sleep she got out of bed and put on her robe. She stood there watching Tyler sleep. For the first time in her life Bracie Turner Shaw knew what hatred felt like. She turned and went to the kitchen.

Tyler got up, showered, and dressed without waking Bracie. They had a rough evening and an even rougher night. He went down to pick up the keys and noticed his CromeMaster knife was out of its block.

"Remind Cora to put it back," he said on his way out the door.

It was still early and only a few of the crew members were at the studio. Shanelle and Kenny saw Tyler coming. The rage resurfaced and they could see it in his eyes. When Greg saw Tyler coming his way, his smile disappeared.

"You sorry, greedy, fool!" Tyler yelled at him. Everyone turned in time to see Tyler reach back and punch Greg.

"Wait, wait!" Greg begged as he crawled away from Tyler.

"It was yours until you tried to hurt my wife!" Tyler yelled at him again. He picked Greg up and punched him again. Greg hit the wall and crumbled to the floor. Tyler reached down to pick him up again. Kenny, Carl, and some of the crewmen ran to Tyler when Shanelle started screaming,

"Get him; get Tyler before he kills him!"

"Get off of me!" Tyler yelled. "Don't touch me! Tell this sorry piece of crap he's fired. Tell him to get his stuff and get out of my studio." Tyler turned to the crew, "Any of this gets out, not only will you not have a job, you will have to answer to me. Is that understood?" he yelled.

No one said anything; they all nodded yes. They had never seen Tyler Shaw angry, but they were all glad to be rid of Greg.

When Greg came to, he got the message and went into his office. Tyler had already ripped his name off the door. He sat behind his desk and turned towards the window. His door opened and closed.

"I'm packing now," he said. When he turned his chair around, Bracie was standing there. Before he could say anything, Bracie swung Tyler's knife across the front of his chest.

"What the …?" he screamed when he saw blood on his shirt.

Bracie seemed to be out of her body, she was feeling so much anger and hatred.

"I told you that if you ever hurt Tyler, I was going to kill you," and she swung at him again.

"Bracie, wait please," he begged.

Meanwhile, Tyler stepped out of his office to apologize to his crew when one of them said to tell Ms. Bracie hello.

"I will when I get home," Tyler said.

"She's here, Mr. Tyler," he said.

"Here, are you sure?"

"Yes sir, I thought she went to your office," he replied.

Tyler remembered the knife out of its block.

"Oh God!" he shouted.

Carl, Kenny, and Shanelle ran behind Tyler.

They could hear Greg outside his door begging Bracie not to hurt him anymore. Tyler pushed the door open slowly and saw the look of fear on Greg's face. He was bleeding and Bracie was holding his knife. She never looked towards Tyler.

"You are a coward, Greg. What's the matter now? You saw me making love to Tyler earlier and you were jealous. You stood there and you watched us, I saw you!" Bracie swung and hit his hand. "You thought I would be like the others? When you found out different, you let that tramp whore into my husband's bed to try to infect us!" she yelled at him.

"Bracie," Tyler called her name softly so he wouldn't startle her.

He looked at Greg and mouthed, "Don't You Move."

Tears started flowing down her face. Tyler knew then she understood he was there.

"Bracie give me the knife, baby," he continued to talk softly to her.

"No Tyler, I told him I would kill him if he ever hurt you!"

Bracie swung at him again and blood started pouring from his arm. Greg was so scared he felt weak.

"Bracie if you kill Greg, he still wins because you won't be with me. Please Angel, listen to my voice, baby. Put down the knife, Bracie." Tyler said more calmly than he felt.

"What?" she asked through her tears.

"I love you, Bracie, I cannot live if you are gone." Tyler kept talking to Bracie as he eased behind her.

Greg wanted to run, but Carl told him again, "Don't Move!" Bracie stood there crying.

"I have never done anything to you," she said to Greg.

"I'm sorry, Bracie. I am so sorry," Greg apologized.

For the first time in a very long time, he told the truth and everyone could tell it.

"Don't do it Bracie; you are better than this," Greg said as tears started to fill his eyes.

"It's not worth it," he said. Greg let the tears fall. And for the first time in his life he felt remorse for all the wrong he had done, especially to Tyler and Bracie.

"Why?" she asked.

"I don't know Bracie, I don't know," Greg dropped his head in shame.

Tyler walked behind Bracie and took the knife. When Bracie realized what she had done, she put her head in Tyler's chest and cried. He held her and rubbed her back.

"It's okay, Angel," he comforted her.

Two of the crewmen stood in the doorway with Kenny and Carl because Shanelle was by Bracie's side.

"Boss, what do you need us to do?" they asked.

"First take this fool to the hospital and get him checked."

"Greg I don't care what kind of story you have to make up, but you better not mention anything that happened here." Tyler told him angrily.

He turned to the crewmen, "I need you to come back and clean this place up spotless."

"Yes sir,"

"Greg, I need to see you here in my office at 8:00am sharp. Do you understand?"

Greg nodded.

"Get him out of here," Tyler said as he continued to hold Bracie.

"I am so sorry he tried to hurt you because of me." Bracie's tears kept streaming down her face.

"Tyler, I didn't do that to his face, I promise I didn't." she said sincerely.

Shanelle started laughing, "No, your husband did!"

"What did you hit him with?" Bracie asked.

Shanelle laughed harder when Carl said, "His fist and he deserved that whipping and some more." Carl looked at his wife and laughed, too.

Tyler turned to Kenny, "I need you to be at my home this afternoon. I will call my lawyer so we can have some legal papers drawn up."

"Yes sir," Kenny answered.

Tyler held on to Bracie and they went home.

Chapter Twenty-seven

Greg had been gone from T. Wahs Production for six years when Tyler got a wedding invitation from him. Bracie chose not to attend, but sent her sincere prayer for their happiness. Her life was truly happy now. Her family came down once a year to celebrate with her in her home. Bracie partnered with Vanessa to open another youth center, and she mentored young ladies between the ages of thirteen and eighteen. Bracie kept to her passion, writing. She put her dreams with Matthew into action, The Master's Peace. Bracie would soon release her fifth book under this umbrella. Tyler was busy with his studio. He produced/directed two hit movies two years in a row. He made time to travel with Bracie to help endorse her books and to hear her speak. As much as Tyler loved Bracie's writing, he loved to hear her speak even more. Bracie's love for God radiated in her life. She was contagious, Tyler always said. They attended church regularly in California now, but Bracie would not change her membership. She went home as much as possible to visit and would stay longer when she had speaking engagements. Tyler and Bracie Shaw were America's favorite couple to watch and read about.

Bracie sat at her desk preparing for her upcoming book release and a seminar she had to teach. Tyler walked in and kissed her.

"What's wrong?" he asked. He could see the frown lines on her face.

"I need you to help me on something," she said.

"What might that be?" Bracie looked at Tyler with a smile, "I would like for you to help me teach this marriage seminar that's coming up," she said and laughed at the look on his face.

"Come on baby, just tell what you believe on love and marriage from the man's point of view."

Tyler never answered, he just looked at her. Bracie got up and walked over to him.

"You can do it baby. Search your heart and tell why you think God made me for you," she said.

"Let me work on that," Tyler told Bracie as they went upstairs together.

Bracie's book release was a success. She sent an autographed copy to Dwayne, for he was now a proud grandfather of two. They kept their promise to stay in touch. Dwayne and Bracie's friendship was bound by an unspoken love

Bracie

that neither could explain. They knew and understood they were placed exactly where God wanted them to be.

Tyler came into Bracie's office and gave her two sheets of paper. She glanced up at him.

"What is this baby?" she asked.

"I did what you asked. I looked into my heart and put into words why I think God made you for me." Tyler stood as she picked up the paper and read it.

Tyler wrote: When I created the heavens and the earth I spoke them into being. When I created man, I formed him and breathed life into his nostrils. But you woman, I fashioned after I breathed the breath of life into man because your nostrils are too delicate. I allowed a deep sleep to come over man so I could patiently and perfectly fashion you. Man was put to sleep so that he could not interfere with my creativity. From one bone I fashioned you. I chose the bone that protects his heart and his lungs and supports him, as you are meant to do. Around this one bone I shaped you, I molded you, I created you perfectly and beautifully. Your characteristics are as the rib, strong yet delicate and fragile. You provide protection for the most delicate organ in man, his heart. His heart is the center of his being and his lungs hold the breath of life. The rib cage will allow itself to be broken before it will allow damage to the heart or lungs. Support your man as the rib cage supports his body. You were not taken from his feet to be under him, nor were you taken from his head to be above him. You were taken from his side to stand beside him and be held close to his side. You are my perfect angel, you are my beautiful daughter. You have grown to be a splendid woman of excellence and my eyes fill when I see the virtues of your heart. Your eyes, don't change them; your lips, how lovely when they part in prayer, your nose so perfect in form; and your hands so gentle in touch. I have caressed your face in your deepest sleep, and I have held your heart close to mine. Adam walked with me into the cool of the day and yet he was lonely. He could not see me or touch me. He could only feel me. So everything I wanted Adam to share and experience with me, I fashioned in you. My holiness, my strength, my purity, my love, my protection, and support I have wrapped in you. You, woman are special because you are the extension of me. Man represents my image, Woman represents my emotions. Together you two represent the totality of Me. So man, treat woman well. Love her and respect her, for she is fragile. In hurting her, you hurt Me. What you do to her, you do to Me. In crushing her, you only damage your own heart and the heart of the Father, You are God's love for me manifested into my wife, my angel, Bracie Shaw. Love Tyler.

Bracie put the paper to her heart as tears ran down her face. "I will teach with you," Tyler said as he took Bracie into his arms. They walked over to the chaise and that is where they spent the night.

Chapter Twenty-eight

Tyler sat on the plane waiting to get home to Bracie. He had been working on site for their last two anniversaries. They finished filming early, and he was on his way home to surprise her. Tyler thought about their last seminar and laughed. He and Bracie had been teaching marriage seminars two and three times a year at different churches all over the U.S. since he taught with her at the first one five years ago. He was at, what seemed to be, the prime of his life. His love for Bracie seemed to grow deeper each year. Bracie had taught him true love, and Tyler believed it was because of her diligence in waiting until they were married to become sexually involved.

Tyler closed his eyes and thought about the evening he heard Bracie praying, "Lord teach me to love Tyler the way that you love Tyler. Help me to see Tyler as the man of God that you see." Bracie, my Bracie, he thought.

Carl met Tyler at the airport. He had already picked up the rose bouquet Tyler ordered.

"Take me to my wife," Tyler chuckled.

Carl dropped Tyler off at the door and headed home.

Cora was coming out of the kitchen when Tyler walked through the door.

"Mr. Tyler!" she said as the glass of water dropped out of her hand. Tyler watched as her face turned pale.

"Where is Bracie?" he asked as he set the flowers on the table.

"What's wrong?" he asked as he ran upstairs.

Tyler stepped into their bedroom not knowing what to expect. The lights were low and Bracie was sleeping. Tyler looked at the clock, and wondered why was she sleeping this time of day? He walked around to her side of the bed and bent to kiss her. Bracie moved and Tyler saw the hospital band on her arm. He stood up and looked around the room and spotted medicine bottles on her vanity.

"What is all of this?" he wondered as he read through the bottles. Tyler pulled up a chair close to the bed and watched Bracie sleep. He wanted to be there when she woke up.

Cora cleaned the spill and went into the kitchen. She looked on the counter and picked up a phone number and the phone. Bracie had been sleep for two hours now and that made Tyler

Bracie

nervous. He heard the doorbell ring and wondered who could be at the door. A few minutes later Cora knocked on the door to inform him that he had a guest. John greeted him at the bottom of the stairs. Tyler shook his hand surprised to see him.

"We need to talk in private," John told him.

They went into Tyler's office and closed the door. John didn't know where to start or what to say. He looked at Tyler

"Bracie is sick, very sick. Tyler, Bracie is dying." Tyler looked at John.

"What did you just say?"

John watched the life drain out of Tyler's face as he explained everything Bracie's doctor told him.

"When did this start, why wasn't I told?" he asked in almost a whisper.

"Bracie got sick about five months ago and went into the hospital. She didn't tell anyone. I'm assuming Cora thought she was in Houston. When she got sick this time it was bad. Dr. McQuintess called me, and I came out right away. I stayed with her for eight days in the hospital, and she has been home for two."

"Why didn't anyone call me?" Tyler yelled from his pain.

John dropped his head, "I wanted to, but she begged me not to. She knew you would leave the filming and come home."

"You are correct, I would have! Bracie is more important to me than any movie!" he yelled again. Tyler paced back and forth in his office. He sat back in front of John.

"Does she need all of that medicine?" he asked.

John nodded his head, but still answered him, "Yes. Tyler, I told Bracie I would tell you as soon as you got home. I thought it would be a week and some days from now. I was on my way home to take care of a few things, and I was coming back. I gave Cora my number and told her to call me if you got in before I got back. She caught me at the airport. Bracie is comfortable. I helped her take her medicines and I bathe her."

Tyler cut him off, "You bathe my wife?" he asked John.

The two men looked at each other, both were hurting. John didn't answer Tyler, he picked up where he left off.

"I bathe Bracie and dress her while Cora changes the linen. She's weak Tyler, but she has to take her medicine. She won't eat most of the time, so do what you can to get her to drink a can of Ensure two or three times a day. Make sure she drinks plenty of fluids so she won't become dehydrated. You will have to help her to the restroom and the doctor says she needs to sit up at least twenty to thirty minutes a day. It does not have to be all at once if she is feeling tired. Tyler, Mama and the children don't know yet. Bracie has been too sick to tell anyone."

John gave Tyler the information to reach Dr. McQuintess. He told Cora to keep his number handy just in case as she walked him to the door. John knew Bracie was in good hands now, he felt better about leaving.

Tyler went back upstairs to watch over Bracie. John's words kept ringing in his head, Bracie is dying. Tyler got his phone and made two calls to Houston.

"Carl will pick you up at the airport," he said and hung up. He called Bracie's doctor and asked if he could be at the house that evening.

"Thank you," Tyler said and hung up the phone. Bracie started waking up and Tyler reached over to help her. Bracie tried to smile at Tyler then asked for help to the bathroom. When she finished, Tyler helped her sit up in bed.

"Why didn't you call me Bracie?"

She looked at him, "I wanted you to finish your movie, Tyler. This could be your biggest movie ever."

"I needed to be with you, Angel. I talked to John and Dr. McQuintess," Tyler told her as tears ran down his face for the first time. Bracie took Tyler into her arms. He put his head on her lap and cried. Bracie rubbed his head and let him cry. Tyler's pain tore at Bracie's heart. She had already cried and there seemed to be no more tears for now, besides she needed her strength for Tyler.

Bracie was resting again, so Tyler went downstairs. Carl came into the house with Ms. Deanie and Anthany. Both knew something was terribly wrong the moment they laid eyes on Tyler. Carl left to get their luggage. He could tell Tyler had been crying and knew something was wrong and it had to do with

Bracie. Tyler told Carl he could leave, but would talk to him and Shanelle later.

"Where is Bracie?" they asked at once.

"She is resting," he said.

The gate buzzer went off. "Please have a seat," he told them as he went to the door. Tyler walked in with Dr. McQuintess and made formal introductions. He sat down and opened his folder and explained Bracie's case.

"At this stage of her illness, conventional medicines are no good; she was too far advanced when she came in five months ago."

"She's been sick for five months and no one knew?" Anthany looked at Tyler.

He shook his head, "I had no idea or I would not have left her here."

Dr. McQuintess explained Bracie has been sick for longer than five months. She kept ignoring symptoms that reappeared regularly. Over the counter medicines made her feel better temporarily, but they were covering up things she should have had checked out. He went on to explain the care Bracie would need at home.

"I do want to check on her while I am here," he said.

All four of them went upstairs. Bracie was sitting up when they entered the room. When she saw her mom and son, tears welled up in her eyes. The doctor let Ms. Deanie and Anthany visit with Bracie as he went over her medicines with Tyler.

Bracie

Bracie asked that her family stay in while the doctor examined her. When he finished, Dr. McQuintess gave them more instructions for Bracie's care.

"Any question?" he asked on his way to the door.

"When can I fly?" asked Bracie.

They all turned and looked at her.

"I need to tell the rest of my family. It's something I must do," she said.

They all looked at the doctor. "As long as you feel strong enough, but please by all means do not over do it. Mrs. Shaw you are very ill and you need to rest as much as possible."

Bracie nods as she turned to get out of bed. Ms. Deanie and Anthany were by her side before her feet touched the floor.

Ms. Deanie sat downstairs with Tyler while Anthany spent time alone watching his mother. He sat there watching her sleep and so many childhood memories came flooding back. Bracie turned to see him sitting there and stretched out her hand to him. Anthany helped her sit up and gave her a hug.

"I love you, Mama," he said softly.

She smiled at him. "I know, son. I love you, too. You have made me very proud. I need you to continue to take care of our family. They look up to you Anthany."

He lay his head on his mother's lap and cried. He never ever thought he would be here without his mother.

Beulah Neveu

A week later, Bracie sat in front of her family at Ms. Deanie's. They knew she was very sick the minute she stepped into the house holding on to Tyler. He explained everything Dr. McQuintess told him in full detail. The house was quiet. D'john walked over to her mother and put her head where Tyler's and Anthany's had been. She cried uncontrollably at the thought of losing her mother. Raymond and Joe'Al kneeled next to her and cried with their sister. Tears ran down Bracie's face as she comforted her children. Tyler stood and watched, but did not interfere, they needed this time together. Bracie called her daughters-in-law over and hugged each one. Andre' came over and knelt next to D'john, while Bracie held his hand. Romesha tried, but was not as strong as she wanted to be. Anthany took her into his arms and let her cry. Bracie's siblings gathered around their mother and shed tears of their own.

Tyler stepped back and looked at Bracie's family as their strength stood out even in this time of adversity. Bracie's love had truly been contagious and now he could really see why.

She reached for Tyler's hand, "I'm tired baby, I need to lay down," she said softly.

All the ladies helped her up and into her bedroom. D'john and Romesha sat by her bedside until she fell asleep. Andre' and Allen sat in disbelief. All the men gathered around Tyler and once again he let his tears flow freely.

Chapter Twenty-nine

Bracie woke up the next morning feeling better than she had in a long time. Tyler was already up and came to her aid.

"I feel okay. I guess the weight of telling the family is off of my shoulders now. I'm glad it's done."

Tyler helped her out of bed and into the restroom. Bracie and Tyler went into the kitchen. Ms. Deanie came in and kissed them both on the cheek.

"I'll have half a cup of coffee and one toast, please," Bracie said to her mom.

She smiled at Bracie and put a full plate of food in front of Tyler. They all laughed when both plates were turned over to Ms. Deanie empty.

"I would like to sit in the front for a while," Bracie told them.

Andre' and D'john broke the news to Trevion, LeAndre' and their wives.

"Grandma is dying!" they said.

Trevion sat in shock, while LeAndre' broke down. Andre' and D'john knew their sons' pain.

"Yes, but you have to get yourself together before you go to see her. She is weak and we don't want her to be upset," Andre' told his sons.

Meanwhile Anthany and Romesha were giving the news to their children. Anthany had to put Necia to bed, she didn't handle the news well at all. The head of each family called their families together and broke the news. Ms. Deanie called their pastors before she left California. John told Bracie and Tyler he would tell Sheila and Dianne because he knew the news would be hard on both of them.

Bracie was still in the front, but lying down. She had quite a few visits from her family and friends. Pastor Roland came by and prayed with Tyler and Bracie. She was tired, but her spirits were up. Tyler brought Bracie her medicines and a light meal. He was glad to see her eat, no matter how small it was. Tyler knew the medicine would make her sleep so he put her to bed. He got a chair and sat next to the bed.

"Tyler, we left home without telling anyone there." Bracie said. "I've been thinking about that," he replied.

Bracie was asleep before Tyler could say anything else.

Bracie

The week went by fast, but Bracie was ready to go home. They informed everyone at Sunday dinner that they would be going home Tuesday afternoon.

Bracie sat in the midst of her family and friends with Tyler by her side. She smiled at her family.

"I know this has been hard on everyone, but I am fine. I have not asked for extra time here on earth, because God has blessed me with a wonderful life. I had a beautiful marriage with Matthew, and before I gave up on love, God blessed me with Tyler. I have always had the love and support of my family and friends. I have grown up and matured spiritually under the greatest duo God put here on earth, my pastors. I have been blessed with wonderful friends here and in California. I have been blessed to be a mother, grandmother, and now a great grandmother. I leave 'The Master's Peace' here for you. I pray my greatest legacy to you all was the life I lived for Jesus Christ. I have not been perfect, but I have loved with all my heart. You know I have always said "Tears cried in faith give you strength." So cry, but please don't grieve too long. I ask that you live life to the fullest. Thank you for loving me and for allowing me to love you."

Bracie could see the tears, and she wanted to bring life to the room. She turned towards Tyler and kissed him on the lips.

"For all the years everyone teased me about Tyler, Ah haa, I gotcha!"

Everyone in the room laughed.

"It has been wonderful, and it has been fun." Bracie said as she held Tyler's hand. "Now can we have some cake, it is for our anniversary."

Everyone got up and hugged Tyler and Bracie and wished them a happy anniversary.

Jekeith walked over to Bracie and she kissed him on the head as usual.

"Grandma, you are going to heaven?" he asked with tears in his eyes.

Bracie smiled through her tears.

"Yes baby, grandma is going to heaven soon."

Bracie looked at Andre'. "He understands I'm dying."

"It seems that way. I'll tell D'john later." he said. Because Bracie was too sick to attend church a lot of the members stopped by to visit. Ms. Deanie' house was full of plants and flowers.

That night, Bracie lay in Tyler's arms. She kissed him softly as she caressed his face. Tyler could tell he was becoming affected by her touch. Bracie knew her touch affected him, because she could feel it. Tyler kissed Bracie and moved her hand from his face.

"You are tired, Bracie, go to sleep," he said.

Bracie put her hand down and lay in his arms, but sleep was the furthest thing from both of their minds.

Bracie

By the time Bracie woke up, Tyler was dressed and gone. She sat up in bed and looked for a book to read. Ms. Deanie came in and helped her freshen up.

"Would you like to eat now or later when you take your medicine?" she asked Bracie.

"Later," she replied.

"Here is some juice, no coffee for you today."

"Yes ma'am," Bracie chuckled with her mother.

Bracie picked up her phone and called Dwayne. Half an hour later Ms. Deanie told Bracie he was there. Dwayne entered her room and pulled up a chair.

"Bracie, my sweetie, what's wrong?"

Bracie took his hand and told him everything. Dwayne got out of the chair and sat next to her on the bed. He held one hand and caressed her face with the other as tears ran down his face. They both sat in silence for a moment.

"I love you, Bracie. I could never explain it, but…"

She smiled at him. "I understand Dwayne. I have loved you all my life. God knew the love would always be our bond, but He trusted us to be obedient to the love of our soul mates," she told him.

"I agree," he said as the tears continued to flow. Dwayne held Bracie's face with both hands and kissed her softly on the lips.

"Do you feel strong enough to sit in the front?" he asked, "I think we need to get out of your bedroom."

Dwayne helped Bracie into the living room. They were still laughing and talking when Tyler came in. The men spoke and shook hand.

"It's been a while since we've seen you and the family," Tyler said.

"Yes it has," Dwayne answered.

Tyler knew Bracie had told him she was sick by the look in his eyes. Dwayne shared some of his grandpa moments while they all laughed.

Bracie placed her head on Tyler's shoulder, "I'm tired now, I need to lay down."

Ms. Deanie came in with Bracie's medicine and a light lunch.

"Thank you Mama, can you put it in the room, I'm about to lay down."

Tyler and Dwayne helped Bracie off of the sofa.

She hugged Dwayne and told him softly, "I will see you in Heaven, biker boy."

"For sure," he said. Dwayne gave Tyler a hug and told him he would be praying for them. Dwayne hugged Ms. Deanie when they walked outside.

"Are you going to be okay?" She asked him.

"Yes ma'am," he lied.

Bracie

Dwayne got in his car and drove down the street. He pulled into a church, lay his head on the steering wheel, and cried, for he would not see Bracie's smile or hear her laughter anymore.

Bracie was exhausted after Dwayne's visit. She knew her body was tired, but wanted to spend as much time as she could with him in their last visit together. Tyler helped Bracie with her medicine and her food. The medicine combined with exhaustion, and it didn't take her long to start dozing off.

She took Tyler's hand. "Where is Sheila?" she asked.

"She will come before we leave tomorrow, now go to sleep." Tyler kissed her on the cheek as she went on to sleep.

Ms. Deanie sat at the table with her head down. Tyler turned to leave out of the room when she informed him that she was not asleep. Tyler's face was worn with worry and concern.

"She's asking for Sheila again?"

Tyler looked at Ms. Deanie.

"She is devastated. I went by there to see her today, and she is in bad shape. I think Bracie is handling this better than most of our family and friends." Tyler said. "Mama, I love Bracie. I don't know how I'm going to make it without her," he said trying not to cry again.

Ms. Deanie patted Tyler on the hand, "By God's grace and strength we will get through this."

He heard her, but he still wasn't convinced. Life without Bracie was something he didn't think would be possible. Ms. Deanie stood up.

"Let me get dinner started," she said as she walked into the kitchen with tears in her eyes.

Bracie was up early that day, but was still tired. Tyler sat her up in bed and helped her eat a bowl of yogurt with toast.

"Drink the juice, Bracie," he was teasing as Sheila knocked on the door and walked in.

When she saw how weak Bracie was, she started crying. Tyler looked at Sheila and told her to come over.

"I'll leave you two alone for awhile," he said on his way out the door.

Tyler wondered how in the world could she produce more tears after their visit today. Bracie and Sheila hugged each other and cried together. They laughed and talked about a lot of things from Matthew and Daniel to their lives now. She gave Bracie a small photo book of Shani.

"She is getting so big," Bracie said as she smiled at her goddaughter's pictures.

"She is a little lady," Sheila replied.

Bracie started feeling weak and lay her head back against the bed.

"You tired?" Sheila asked.

Bracie only nodded.

Bracie

Sheila kissed her on the forehead.

"I'll send Tyler in, and Bracie, how in God's name can you look so beautiful at a time like this?"

Bracie smiled. Sheila got what she wanted, a smile to remember.

"I love you my friend, my sister," Sheila said as she left to go get Tyler.

Tyler bathed and dressed Bracie and put her to bed. There was a knock on the door.

"Come in," Tyler said. Trevion, LeAndre, and DeShaun walked in.

"Hey grandma," they all said.

Bracie looked and told them to come closer to the bed. They each gave her a hug.

"We love you, grandma, and we are going to miss you. We promise to raise our children and teach them like you did us," they said.

"Wonderful," she said. "Remember what grandma always told you, God gave men tear ducts, too. It's okay to use them."

LeAndre' began to tear up and Trevion playfully pushed him out of the way. DeShaun sat on the bed and held his grandmother's hand. He didn't say anything, he just held her hand. He reached up and kissed his grandmother on the forehead.

"Grandma is fine, you just remember what I said, okay?"

Trevion's wife came in with their daughter. Jr. was walking behind her. When he saw Bracie he ran and jumped into her arms. Bracie took her great granddaughter into her arms.

"She is so beautiful."

"Do you feel like taking a few pictures with her?" asked Trevion.

"Sure!" said Bracie as her face lit up.

Her grandsons laughed, "Still ready to take pictures on a dime, huh?"

After taking a few pictures, Ms. Deanie and D'john walked in.

"Let us take our generation picture," Ms. Deanie said.

They were all taking pictures. Bracie was smiling, but Tyler could tell she was very tired. By the time he got to the bed, Bracie had tears flowing down her face.

"I'm sorry everyone, but I think that's enough for tonight." Bracie asked for LeAndre'. He walked over to her side and wiped her tears.

"Tell my great grandbaby about me when she is born. Promise me you will. Kiss your wife for me," she told him.

"I promise, Grandma," he said with tears in his eyes again.

She hugged him and reached for Tyler. That night Tyler held Bracie in his arms. She went to sleep on his chest.

Chapter Thirty

Bracie was glad to be home in her own bed. Tyler let her rest for a few days before calling their friends over. Josh & Vanessa, Larry & Gail, and Kenny & Sondra were in the sitting room when Carl and Shanelle came in. Shanelle knew Bracie was sick, but she had no idea how serious.

"Tyler is getting Bracie," said Sondra. They all looked at the chair in the center of the room because it had several bed pillows in it. Bracie had gotten so small, Tyler was packing her like a child. He brought her in and sat her in the chair. Shanelle grabbed hold of Carl and started crying before Tyler said anything. Tears were in everyone's eyes as Tyler made sure Bracie was comfortable. Bracie held Tyler's hand as he told everyone about her illness. Bracie expected the crying, but she felt so bad for Shanelle.

"Come to me," she beckoned.

Carl helped Shanelle over to Bracie. This time Bracie held her and let her cry.

As hard as Tyler tried to keep Bracie's health from getting into the media, it did. Their picture was in every major newspaper and magazine in America. Tyler didn't usually read any of them, but he wanted to be sure Bracie's name was not mishandled by the press. After he read through several, he called Shanelle to come over to the house because he never left now.

Shanelle came over right away. She and Carl rushed in and Tyler had to get her to calm down so he could explain what he wanted. He divided the magazines and papers between the three of them.

"Every one that has a good story place it here on this table."

When they finished, all of the articles were placed on the table.

"Will you send a thank you card to each editor for the kind story they wrote on Bracie?" he asked.

"Yes, I will get on it today. Can I go see Bracie?" she asked while getting up.

Tyler opened the door for Kenny and some of the crewmen. Bracie and Tyler had received hundreds of cards and letters at the production studio. Kenny told Tyler the studio looked like a flower shop, a huge flower shop. Tyler asked Shanelle and Vanessa to donate the flowers to local hospitals, charities, and shelters. He only asked for every card be taken from the flowers and be brought to him. Tyler felt good that so many people cared about his wife. When she was awake and feeling well Tyler would read some of the many cards and letters they received. Bracie was getting weaker and there was nothing he could do to change it. Tyler lay in bed watching over her. Bracie stirred and he sat up to make sure she was comfortable. As soon as Tyler lay back down, Bracie instantly moved into his arms. He kissed the top of her head and eventually went to sleep.

Bracie was up early. She wanted to sit in the garden. Cora brought breakfast for Bracie and Tyler outside. Bracie sat close to Tyler so she wouldn't need the pillows. When Tyler felt Bracie was tired, he picked her up and carried her into the house.

"I would like to go to my office, please."

Tyler sat Bracie behind her desk. She touched the box she had especially made to hold Tyler's original papers of *Why God Made Her For Him*. Bracie asked Tyler to get the first three scrapbooks she made of them. He pulled up a chair and he and Bracie went through each book. He took their wedding album upstairs. Bracie laid in Tyler's arms as they looked at the pictures. Bracie lay her head back and Tyler ran his fingers through her hair over and over.

"Your hair is beautiful, my angel," he said.

It was still thick, beautiful, and healthy. Bracie smiled at Tyler and went to sleep. He laid her on her pillows and put their wedding album on her vanity.

Tyler and Bracie were home for about two weeks when she stopped eating again. She would barely drink a can of Ensure, but she continued to drink water and juice. She started sleeping a lot more. Shanelle and Vanessa would take turns sitting with Bracie during the day while Tyler worked downstairs or took a nap. One afternoon Bracie took off her angel pendant and gave it to Shanelle.

"How quickly can you have this duplicated?" she asked.

"In a few days, why," Shanelle asked. "I want the original to go to Necia and I want to be buried in the duplicate."

Shanelle looked at Bracie. "Don't cry sister, please. Get this done for me ASAP."

Shanelle kissed Bracie and went to the jeweler's. Bracie sat up for awhile longer and looked around the room. She thanked God for blessing her so richly.

Bracie watched Tyler as he moved around the room. He was taking very good care of her, and she appreciated it. When Tyler realized she was awake, he sat by her on the bed.

"Bracie do you want me to move into another room so you can sleep better?" he asked.

She looked at him. "Is that the real reason you want to leave our bed?" she asked as tears filled her eyes.

Bracie

"What are you talking about Bracie?"

"I tried to kiss you at Mama's, and you pushed me away. I was awake a few times when you were in the shower."

Tyler looked at Bracie because he never thought she knew what he was doing.

"I know I have lost a lot of weight and I may not be as pretty and healthy as I used to be, but it hurts to know that you don't desire to be with me anymore," she said crying.

Tyler was shocked at Bracie's words.

"No baby, that's not true. My angel, I did not want to hurt you. You are weak, Bracie; I didn't want you to think I was being insensitive to you right now."

Bracie caressed Tyler's face, "What I want right now is my husband," she said.

Tyler kissed Bracie for the first time in over a month. When Bracie slid her hand behind his head Tyler's body came to life and so did Bracie's. Tyler was still afraid of hurting her, but he needed to let her know she was wanted, desired, and loved. Every time he touched her, Bracie called his name out softly.

"Bracie are you ok?" he asked nervously.

She touched his face, "Yes baby, I am fine, thank you Tyler."

"The pleasure was all mine," he said.

Bracie laughed and said, "No, not all of it."

Tyler laughed at her humor. He lay down and took Bracie into his arms. She was resting well. When Tyler was sure Bracie was asleep, he went to take a cold shower.

Bracie woke up radiant. She lay in Tyler's arms and spent hours sharing intimacy in their marriage that they both had been missing.

Tyler looked down at Bracie, "Angel, how in the world can you still kiss me and turn me on so?"

"It's love my dear; it's a gift God gave us a long time ago," she smiled up at him and kissed him again.

Bracie's illness continued to make her weak, but it did not take away the glow that Tyler's love put on her face. Bracie talked to her mom and children every day that she was strong enough to. Ms. Deanie told Bracie she was packing up to come out there with her. That made Bracie happy for she wanted to be with her mom as much as possible now.

When Shanelle brought the pendant back a few days later, Ms. Deanie walked into the bedroom with her. Bracie was so glad to see her mother. She asked Ms. Deanie to put the duplicate angel on her neck while Shanelle got Tyler. Bracie could barely sit up alone. Ms. Deanie and Tyler helped prop her up on the bed pillows.

"Baby, bring me my jewelry drawer and put it here," she said patting the bed next to her.

"I need the blue bag off of my vanity also, please."

Tyler noticed it a few times, but never thought to look in it. Bracie took out a list and small hand written gift cards.

"Open all the boxes," she said. "Put the card in the jewelry box that I tell you and pass them out at Mama's after my funeral, at Sunday dinner. She gave each of her four granddaughters a special pendant of hers. She also gave Necia the bracelet to match her pendant. Next came her only daughter, then her daughters-in-law. Bracie picked up the emerald necklace, her first gift from Tyler.

"This is for my first great granddaughter." She chose a ruby and diamond necklace for her great-granddaughter that had not been born yet. Bracie reached over and gave her mother her favorite pearls Tyler had given her on their sixth wedding anniversary. Bracie had everything chosen and well written out. When she fell asleep, Shanelle, Tyler, and Ms. Deanie finished putting the jewelry as she wanted. When they got to the bottom of the note, they both laughed, because she had written, "Now give the bag to Carl. You two will be in no shape to do any of this and stop laughing cause you know I'm telling the truth," which made them laugh all the more.

"Still got that sense of humor," Shanelle said.

She hugged Tyler and Ms. Deanie and left.

After a few more days, Bracie started refusing her medicines. She only wanted to sleep now. Tyler called Dr.

McQuintess to come over and examine Bracie. Ms. Deanie and Tyler were standing there as he looked at Bracie.

"She is nearing the end, son. She will sleep without the medicines now and she seems to be in no pain."

"How long will this take?" Tyler asked in tears again.

"A few days, a week it's up to her mostly. When she passes call me and not 911. Mrs. Shaw is considered at home hospice."

Tyler shook his hand and asked Cora to show the doctor out. Tyler and Ms. Deanie sat by her bed each day now. He rarely left their room.

One afternoon Cora informed Tyler that he had guests. Ms. Deanie sat with Bracie while he went downstairs. All of their friends were there to offer what help they could. Tyler gave them the news and thanked them for coming. He went to his office to make a few phone calls. Tyler called their children and told them they would have tickets paid and ready to go tomorrow morning. Tyler told Ms. Deanie she could go to bed, because he would be with Bracie for the rest of the night. He walked her to her bedroom and went downstairs.

When he came back he thought Bracie had slid out of bed, then he could see that she was praying. He stepped back out so she could have her time with the Father.

"*My Father, I know I am about to be home soon. I look forward to it with great anticipation. I am not asking to stay any longer here on earth, but what I would like is strength. Will you give me strength to make love with Tyler one more time? Please*

Lord, we both need it, we really do. Right now, I can barely move and my body is weak. Father you already know Tyler will not do it if he thinks I am too weak. Please let me make love to him again, it's just my way of saying thank you for loving me enough to wait all those years ago and for loving through the years. Please Father, Amen."

Bracie knew before she said amen that God answered her prayer. She got up slowly, but she was strong enough to stand alone. She walked to the bathroom and showered. Bracie moved slowly to the closet and put on her white gown. It was big now, but it would work. Tyler knew he heard water running. When he got to the top of the stairs he could smell Bracie's Forever Butterfly.

Tyler walked into the room and was taken aback when he saw how beautiful Bracie looked sitting on the chair with the lights turned low. She stood up and walked to the stereo.

"The Wedding Song," he whispered. "Let me shower first," he said as he walked into the bathroom. When Tyler came out, Bracie walked over and removed his towel.

" I love you, Bracie," he said in her ear.

She kissed Tyler with the passion they shared before she became sick. Every move he made was intentionally slow. He had to hold on to this night, this moment. Tyler picked Bracie up and carried her to their bed. He sat her down and kissed her face. Bracie caressed and kissed Tyler slowly over his face.

"That feels good, Tyler," she kept saying.

Bracie's body could not be still.

"Make love to me, Tyler; make love to me," Bracie said between breaths.

She looked at Tyler and smiled. Tyler put his hand to her heart.

"I love you, Tyler," Bracie said through tears. "Always know I love you."

"Love me, Tyler," she cried softly.

Tyler watched Bracie. He tried to kiss every tear that rolled down her face.

"I love you, Bracie," he said. "Oh my angel I love you."

Tyler put Bracie's hand to his heart as he gave in to her. They both lay there in each other's arms.

Tyler got up, "Can you shower?" he asked.

Bracie nodded. Tyler helped her into the shower. Once Bracie was clean, she told Tyler she needed to sit down. He helped her dry off.

"I'm cold, Tyler. I need a regular gown," she said.

Tyler sat her at the vanity. He put her gown on her and brushed her hair into a ponytail. He watched her in the mirror as she looked at their wedding album. She flipped to a picture with just the two of them on it.

"This is my favorite picture," she told Tyler, as he glanced over her shoulder.

"Really, even after looking at it hang downstairs for eleven years."

"Yep, even after all this time," she said.

Tyler helped Bracie into bed. She was asleep by the time he pulled the covers over her.

When Tyler got up the next morning, he expected to see Bracie awake with new energy. He reached over and touched her. Bracie's skin was cool and clammy.

"Bracie!" he shouted as he jumped out of bed. "Bracie, baby please open your eyes," Tyler cried. Bracie touched his hand and barely opened her eyes. He grabbed the phone and called Dr. McQuintess. Tyler went to get Ms. Deanie. Tyler got dressed and ran downstairs when the buzzer went off on the gate. He let the doctor in and was about to close the door when John drove up to the gate. He sent the doctor upstairs with Ms. Deanie and Bracie as he waited for John. He told him what happened that morning as they walked upstairs. They walked into the bedroom while Dr. McQuintess was still examining Bracie. When he finished Dr. McQuintess shook hands with John.

"Mr. Wright?" he asked.

John simply said "Yes."

The doctor turned to Tyler and Ms. Deanie, "It's only a matter of time now. Her pressure is dropping and so is her body temperature. It could be a few hours, but no more than a day at the most. John walked the doctor downstairs. I will send over a nurse as soon as possible. She will stay until Mrs. Shaw passes away." He said. John thanked him and went back upstairs as Cora showed the doctor out.

Tyler was at Bracie's side. "Angel hold on, the children are on their way here." John and Ms. Deanie watched Tyler, his face looked as pale as Bracie's. Tyler was able to call Carl and give him all the flight information. Shanelle came to the house and went straight to Bracie's side. John stood there, the one place he did not want to be right now, was Houston. He knew Bracie's family would not be handling this last news well. Everyone loved Bracie, she was all heart. Ms. Deanie, Tyler, and John did not leave Bracie's side.

Tyler and Bracie's bedroom was filled with their family by late afternoon. Ms. Deanie kneeled by Bracie's bedside and touched her hand.

"Mama is still here," she said. "Bracie, the kids are here."

Her eyelids fluttered, but did not open. Carl went downstairs and got chairs for everyone. They all sit there mostly in silence. Bracie stirred later that evening and Tyler moved by her side. Bracie opened her eyes and tried to smile. Her family looked at her and smiled through their tears.

"John, did I hear John?" she asked softly.

He stepped over to Bracie and held her hand. "Take care of Tyler for me. Thank you for always being there for me. I know you came to talk to Tyler all those years ago."

Bracie

John and Tyler smiled through their tears. Bracie kissed each one of her children and Shanelle.

She looked at Tyler and smiled, "I'm tired baby," Bracie said as she went back to sleep.

They all sat there not knowing what to say or do, but they did not move. At 11:30pm, Bracie opened her eyes again and asked for Tyler.

"I'm right here my angel," he told her.

"Hold me, Tyler," she asked him. He took Bracie in his arms.

"The prayer last night was for you," she whispered in his ear.

"For me?" he asked confused at first.

"Yes Tyler," she said with a smile.

"You prayed for strength to make love to me?" he asked through his tears.

"Yes," she said softly.

Everyone knew they were talking to each other, but could not hear what they were saying.

Bracie lay her head in Tyler's chest, "I love you Tyler. I'm ready to go home now," she said.

Bracie hugged Tyler back.

At 11:42 p.m., Bracie's arms fell softly to her lap and she went home to be with the Lord, while Tyler rocked her in his arms. They all stood around Tyler while he cried with Bracie still in his arms. D'john, Romesha, and Shanelle held Bracie while her sons picked Tyler up and carried him from the room. The nurse came in and did the final exam and pronounced Bracie Turner Shaw, dead at 11:52 pm.

Epilogue

Bracie's funeral was beautiful, but very sad. It was attended by people from all over the United States. Bracie's family was shocked to see the church was filled to capacity, with two over flow rooms added to accommodate the people. Flowers covered the entire front of the church. Tyler saw nothing, but the pearl casket that held Bracie. When the funeral director closed the casket, Tyler wanted to die with Bracie. He vaguely remembered being at the cemetery. Tyler went to Ms. Deanie's and sat in the bedroom he shared with Bracie. By the time Carl and Shanelle found him, Tyler was laying across the bed asleep with his suit still on.

Bracie had been gone for over a month, and Tyler still would not leave their home. He stood over Bracie's vanity and stared at their wedding album. It was still turned to Bracie's favorite picture. He wouldn't turn the page or close it. Tyler would sit in their room and listen to her favorite CD's. Carl and Shanelle became very concerned. Tyler was grieving hard, and he seemed to have lost interest in everything and everyone around him.

Tyler sat on their bed and took out the note card Bracie left on the counter for him eleven years ago. *Tonight we shall become one.* Tyler thought about how he and Bracie made love that night. Tears ran down Tyler's face as he lay down and put his hand on his heart.

"I love you Bracie, forever one," Tyler said as he closed his eyes.

Love Is Like

Like the wings of an eagle

that soars in the sky. Like the stillness

of a spring in the sweet by and by.

Like the song of a canary

so soft and so sweet. Like the feel of a

baby so tender and so meek.

Like the protection of a bear

of her young playing cub. Like the tenderness of a mother

giving her child a hug.

Like the excitement of a champion

who has just won first place. Like the innocence of a child

with a smile on his face.

Like the trusting and surrendering of a pure white dove.

Like the beating of my heart

shall you have the depths of my love.